sabotage

CHRONICLES
of NICK:
SHADOWS OF FIRE

SHERRILYN KENYON

OLIVERHEBERBOOKS

Cover Design Copyright © Dar Albert Wicked Smart Designs

Printed in the United States of America

Published by Oliver-Heber Books

0 9 8 7 6 5 4 3 2 1

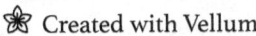 Created with Vellum

PROLOGUE
MOUNT OLYMPUS, 2000

Nekoda Kennedy had been born Nyria Belami Anaxkolasi. Daughter of a justice goddess and a Chthonian father who had been charged with helping to protect mankind from gods who abused their powers.

Protecting the world from those who treated humanity as if people were nothing save pawns to be toyed with and preyed upon. Her father's sacred duty had been to make sure mankind remained safe from predators, regardless of where those predators originated.

Demon, human, gods... it mattered naught.

Her mother had been charged with punishing those who did wrong. Anyone who preyed on the innocent and destroyed their hope. Their futures.

Or took the lives of others.

As her mother used to say, she preferred punishing those who preyed, and especially those who betrayed.

Nyria had learned justice on her parents' knees and felt an insatiable hunger for it deep inside her soul.

An all-consuming need to have order restored to the universe. To never allow anyone to prey on someone else.

Which was why, after her brutal death, Nyria had agreed to return to life to kill the Malachai demon before it had a chance to destroy the world. To take everyone she loved from her.

Everyone.

But plans were never so simple. Nor did they often go without hiccups. The sacred order that had brought her back to life to battle the Malachai had withheld vital information about her life and rebirth.

Vital information such as the fact that the Ambrose Malachai— the very demon they'd ordered her to kill— was, in fact, her husband.

Why? Because they thought their lies justified their cruelty, and like any soulless villain, they didn't care what it did to her life or family.

What it did to the world.

All that mattered was what *they* wanted.

Blinded to consequence, they'd failed to tell her that

one day, she would fight side by side with the Ambrose Malachai to put down the Cyprian Malachai as they tried to save the world from Cyprian's madness.

Even worse? They had done their best to manipulate her with their lies. Lies that had caused her second death.

The only difference was the second time her life had been sacrificed, that death had awakened a need for vengeance unlike anything she'd known before. A craving so strong that it had echoed through the heavens to Mount Olympus where her "aunt," Artemis, lived.

The moment her aunt had heard that distinctive sound of anguished grief borne from utter betrayal, Artemis had come to Kody in her full, towering beauty. With long auburn hair and deep green eyes, she was one of the most beautiful women Kody had ever seen. As always, she'd worn a white dress that hugged every one of her luscious curves.

Bemused, Artemis had stared at Kody with a stern frown. "I feel like I know you, but I don't. But I do, don't I?"

In her spirit form, Kody smiled. "You know me, Aunt Artie... in the future."

Her frown deepening, Artemis had approached her cautiously. "You are Bethany's child?"

Kody nodded. "I need you to use Acheron's powers to restore me to life. Please!" As the identical twin to Kody's father, Acheron was her uncle, the father of Artemis's daughter.

Born an Atlantean god of final fate, Acheron had the power over life and death. There was almost nothing he couldn't do. And because he'd once shared blood with Artemis, she held a lot of the powers that Acheron wielded.

If Artemis wanted, she could easily bring Kody back to life the same way Artemis revived the Dark-Hunters who served her. Like Kody, Dark-Hunters died from a betrayal that was so agonizing, they bargained their eternal service and souls to Artemis for a single Act of Vengeance against those who'd done them wrong.

Even so, Artemis had hesitated. "I don't know... Acheron loses his shoulder whenever I bring people forward."

Kody barely stopped herself from laughing as she remembered the one thing about Artemis that annoyed Acheron beyond endurance.

Her aunt could never get any saying right. She always butchered any and all idioms. Most of the time, she did so by accident. But there were times when Kody knew her aunt did it simply to annoy Acheron.

And others.

"Please, Aunt Artie, I have to save Nick Gautier."

Artemis's green eyes flared at the mention of Nick's name. At this point in time, Artemis had no idea what Nick would one day come to mean to her, personally. Nick was not only integral to Kody's life, but Artemis's, too. "That annoying little brat Acheron favors? The one who thinks he's charming when he's a toad in a tacky shirt?"

Kody nodded. Acheron and Nick were very distant cousins. Nick's great-great-some-unbelievably-long-ago-great-ancestor had been an older brother to Acheron. Her belief was that somehow Acheron had sensed that blood connection to Nick the moment they'd met and had been protective over him ever since.

Tacky clothes and all.

It was the only way to explain the way Acheron had bonded so tightly to Nick when he normally shunned being close to anyone else.

Especially those he believed to be human, as they had a nasty tendency to die after a handful of decades while Acheron counted his age in millennia.

Yet in spite of it all, Acheron had allowed Nick's charms to beguile him even quicker than Kody had. Irritating though he could be, Nick was a hard person not to adore.

In the not-so-distant future from now, Artemis would be even more protective over Nick.

Unaware of that future and the truth Kody knew, Artemis stepped back with a pout. "Oh... Acheron would be exceptionally mad if anything happened to that boy. He gets so very cross when the humans he likes die..." She cast a fretful stare at Kody. "Fine. I will bring you back to life. Please, do not tell Acheron what I did. He doesn't need to know I used his powers again. That, too, makes him rather angry."

Kody tapped her heart. "Promise. Not a word. I would never intentionally get you into trouble." She loved Artemis too much for that.

Nodding, Artemis stepped forward and cupped Kody's face. "I feel you are important to me. I don't know why."

Because in the future, she would protect Artemis and her daughter and grandchildren. Artemis's son-in-law would die by Kody's side as they fought as hard as they could to save mankind, and everyone they loved.

It was one of a million memories Kody wished she didn't have. Maybe that was the one gift the Arelim had given her when they'd brought her back with stripped memories. She'd had no idea exactly what lay ahead for her.

Now, she did.

Hindsight's twenty-twenty.

Foresight, too.

And she intended to use that knowledge for everything it was worth.

I will not fail.

I will not falter.

She had too much to lose.

Artemis leaned forward and kissed her forehead. A surge of power went through Kody as she felt her uncle's powers embracing and invading her body. It, too, was like a warm hug.

Acheron...

He had been with her since the moment of her birth. Always there, always laughing and helping her parents. Him and his wife, Tory, and their kids...

So many wonderful memories.

So many nightmares.

With a gasp, she threw her head back and cried out. Birth, even rebirth, was always painful. It felt as if her entire body was being ripped to shreds. Scrubbed raw with a scouring pad. Her very soul screamed from the pain of it all.

Fire ran through her veins, pounding with such ferocity, she was sure she'd die again.

Then suddenly, it stopped.

No pain. No sound.

Nothing.

Still shaking, she lay curled in a ball at Artemis's feet. Honestly, she was too scared to move for fear it might bring the pain back to her.

The Greek goddess knelt down to brush her dark hair from her forehead. "Are you all right?"

Kody nodded even though she wasn't completely sure. The way she felt, she didn't know if she'd ever be okay again.

Everything was so wrong. They'd lost their battle. Their enemies had won.

She'd died.

Her friends needed her.

If they didn't stop Cyprian, the world wouldn't survive the nightmare he intended to bring. So very much was wrong.

But the longer she lay there, unmoving, the more those fears faded.

And took with it all the pain and uncertainty. The nightmares that haunted her while awake and sleeping. A sudden tranquility wrapped around her and left her feeling as if she were inside a warm cocoon.

There was no more fear. No pain. Instead, raw determination took root and revived her.

This wasn't the end. It was half time. There was a lot

more left to the game. Cyprian believed her to be side-lined. But it was time for a huddle.

A new plan that wouldn't fail.

One they wouldn't see coming.

Artemis held a long, graceful hand out to her.

Kody took it without hesitation and allowed the goddess to pull her to her feet.

As she rose, she wasn't sure what to expect. It'd taken her forever to get used to the first body she'd been brought back in. While some of it had been familiar, most of it had been like wearing a Halloween costume from someone else.

Heck, she'd even flinched a few times when she caught sight of her reflection. The Arelim had returned her to life in a body so alien and foreign that it'd figuratively itched.

But this time... She looked down at her hands and saw the same rosy beige skin tone she'd been born with. In fact, her hands were completely familiar. Her height, too.

Smiling, Artemis manifested a mirror to show her what she looked like. "Is this what you wanted?"

Dear Lord...

It *was* her.

How? How was this possible?

Stunned and grateful, Kody stared at the visage of

someone she knew intimately. Not the reflection of a stranger.

It was *her* face!

Those same greenish-gold eyes that were identical to her mother's set in a heat-shaped face framed with her curly black hair. She saw both of her parents' heritage mixed in her features. Her mother's unusual eyes. Her father's strong chin and slight dimples.

Gods, how she'd missed seeing that. Feeling the eternal connection to her family. And she loved seeing their genes reflected back at her again.

Though she'd never reached the height of her parents or brothers, she was still taller than most.

Artemis lowered the mirror. "You look just like her."

"Pardon?"

"Bethany. She's the only one who ever set my brother back on his shins. You've no idea how much I loved your mother for that. You look so much like her that it's as if she's been returned from Apollymi's wrath."

Screwed-up idiom aside, Kody took that as the world's greatest compliment even though it reminded her that in this time period, her mother was a prisoner trapped in stone.

Artemis dissolved the mirror, then held her hand out to manifest a bow.

No, not any bow.

This one had belonged to Kody's mother.

"Take Warbringer and do your mother proud."

Elated, Kody rose up, onto her toes and hugged Artemis. "Thank you! Thank you so much!"

Tears welled in Artemis's eyes. "My pleasure, little one. I wish you luck."

And with that, she vanished and left Kody alone.

Sad to see her aunt go, Kody tightened her grip on the bow. "Please let my powers work... please." Leaning against the bow, she closed her eyes and tapped what she hoped hadn't been stripped from her or bound by an enemy.

If they were to succeed, she'd need every advantage. Those inherited powers...

Her birthright. She wanted to have them back almost as much as she needed Nick.

Yet as she waited, she felt nothing.

No... no! This couldn't be. She had to be able to fight on a level field. Those powers were necessary.

What if she never felt them again?

Tears began to prick at her eyes. It was like losing a member of her family. Surely, she couldn't be human.

Then something changed...

Could it be? She held her breath, counting her heartbeats as hope rose within her.

After a few more terrifying seconds, that old familiar sizzle began deep in her blood.

With a wicked rush that left her breathless, her powers engulfed her like a mother's embrace. The force of it was so intense and overwhelming, she staggered back two feet.

How could she ever have forgotten the feel of this? Every inch of her body was electrified. Charged.

Letting those powers flow all through her, she held her hand out and willed herself to New Orleans.

CALEB MALPHAS WAS one of the surliest demons ever born. The son of a god and a chaos demon, he'd been condemned by all for falling in love with a human and switching sides in the Primus Bellum— the first war of the gods.

From bad to good. As if switching to the right side had been the wrong move. But then given Caleb's past violence and misdeeds that he'd glorified in, no one could or would believe such a ferocious demon, even one in love, could ever give up his wickedness to fight for decency.

It defied credibility.

And so Caleb had lost everything in that battle.

Even the love who'd changed him for eternity and restored a heart he'd never known existed.

Worse, he'd been rejected by all. Evil and good. Neither side trusted him. No one had any use for him.

Until Kody's mother, Bethany, had shown him her faith. After the death of Caleb's wife, she'd been the first to see what no one else could... that there was a soul inside the demon. Because of her mother's belief in Caleb's goodness and heart, Bethany had proclaimed Caleb Kody's godfather.

There was more irony there than Kody wanted to think about. And because of Caleb's loyalty and love for her and her mother, he was the one she sought first.

Or at least tried to access.

Frustrated, Kody stood outside his gigantic Greek Revival-style home like a human. Helpless to gain entry without permission.

She growled at the unyielding door. "I forgot his sigils..." He'd given her access in her former body.

In this one...

She was completely locked out. So, Kody was forced to knock on the door of his palatial home like a regular person.

The gall of it all.

Then again, it probably kept her from being eaten by his unfriendly housemates. There was no telling what the hellhound crew would do if she popped into their home unannounced. Neither Caleb nor his companions liked others as a general rule.

They liked uninvited intruders least of all.

Kody pressed the doorbell. A loud howling rang out through the entire house, and through the porch speakers. Wow.

How have I never heard that before?

Because you always popped into the house and never bothered with his doorbell.

Made sense, as did the unorthodox doorbell, now that she thought about it. It sounded like one of his hellhound friends. In the event one of them was in the wrong form when someone rang it, it would disguise their vicious barking. Make a visitor think that he had a morbid sense of humor.

Or a bunch of big-ass dogs.

One thing about Caleb— he was brilliant.

And very offbeat.

Out of nowhere, a voice growled, "What?"

She glanced around the doorstep, trying to locate who was talking to her. The sound hadn't come from the intercom or speakers. Rather, it sounded like the speaker was standing next to her. "Hello?"

"Who are you and what do you want?" There was that deep, demonic growl she knew so well.

Smiling at Caleb's irritated tone, she continued to search for him. "Caleb, it's me... Kody. I need your help."

"You don't look like—" His voice broke off mid-sentence.

One second she was on his doorstep, the next, she was inside his elegant home.

Before she could move or react, a pair of well-muscled arms pulled her against a steely chest. His black hair was a little longer than he normally wore it, but his eyes were the same shade of brown and his face every bit as chiseled.

He held her far too long and cupped her head as a father would a beloved child. There was no mistaking the relief and love in that embrace. When he finally stepped back, he took her chin in his hand. "It is you, right?"

Overwhelmed with happiness and relief, she nodded as tears welled in her eyes. "It's me."

"My God! You look just like your mother now. Back when I first met her. How are you here? You were dead! I saw you die. How are you not dead?"

She smiled at him. "My death was an unfortunate event, but luckily I have friends in the right places."

"Me money's on that rat, Artemis. Simi's right. She is a heifer goddess."

Kody smiled at the sound of Aeron's voice as the

ancient Celtic war god joined them. She moved away from Caleb to hug the tall blond being who was far more handsome than anyone had a right to be. Especially when he smiled and flashed those adorable dimples. "I've missed all of you so much!"

Aeron's arms tightened around her. "Aye, lass. We've all been the sadder without your lovely face to cheer us. You smell better than me companions, too."

Caleb shook his head. "I can't believe you're back, and in what I assume is your real body?"

"Sort of." She scowled. "I'm still kind of confused about it. This is what I looked like as a teenager, not how I looked when I died as an adult. Weird, right?"

"Artemis," Aeron said with a laugh. "Much like idioms, she could never do ages properly. Besides, everything with her is like playing a game of horseshoes."

"Horseshoes?"

"You know, *close enough.*"

Kody laughed at the reference that in horseshoes, it didn't matter if you actually hit the target. It only mattered how close you came to the goal.

Aeron was right. Vintage Artie, as it also explained her lack of ability to say anything correctly.

She glanced between the two of them. "Where's the rest of you?"

Vawn appeared by her side. Tall and thin, he was a

ghostlike wraith many called a banshee. Dressed in black rags, he had long, stringy red hair and dark eyes and lips, with a distinctive tattoo in the center of his forehead— a black, elongated star.

But looks weren't what they seemed. Vawn wasn't always Gwrach y Rhibyn— the hag of the robin. He'd started out in life as a man who'd been cursed into a female body after he broke the heart of a woman and she killed herself over him.

Now, he was forever damned to walk the earth in that same woman's body.

The saddest part? It hadn't been his fault. The woman had preyed upon him and stalked him near to madness. Then, when he refused to return her uninvited and unwanted love, this curse had been her final revenge.

To ensure he'd never forget her.

It was heartbreaking, really.

Vawn was also a constant companion of Kaziel, a cŵn who'd been created by the Celtic gods. His kind were messengers who guarded the gates of Annwn— the Celtic underworld. In a way, cŵns were like banshees, in that anyone who heard their baying was destined to die.

Similar to Vawn, Kaziel had a tattoo in the center of his forehead. Only his was a sun symbol that marked him as being aligned to the side of light, even though he was a creature torn between light and dark. Forever lured between them. Never trusted by either, and cursed by both.

Just like Caleb.

Kaziel had long, pale blond hair that fell to his shoulders. Tiny braids interlaced with beads and feathers held it back from his chiseled, handsome face. And unlike Vawn, he had other facial tattoos that curved from his chin up and over his cheeks in the shape of tusks. They came to a sharp point under eyes that were so light and green they glowed with an ethereal, fey light.

Vawn, Kaziel, and Aeron made up the *Arswyd gan drindod*— terror by a trinity. In battle, they were invincible.

Especially when they were backed by Zavid— one of the highest-level warrior demons. A shapeshifter by birth, he could assume any form he wanted.

But his favorite was that of a black hellhound.

Yeah, Caleb kept company with a scary bunch of friends.

And she loved every one of them. Kody made sure to hug each of them in turn. Then she turned to Caleb, as one of his crew was notably missing. "Where's Xev?"

"Making sure something doesn't eat Nick."

That made sense. As Nick's great-grandfather, Xev had a vested interest in keeping Nick safe.

"Can we call him back?"

Caleb frowned. "Why would we do that? It's so quiet when he's gone." He gave a sarcastic grimace to the group.

Kody laughed, knowing Xev was the quietest one of them all. Even Caleb talked more. "You're awful."

"That's what they tell me." Pulling out his phone, he called Xev.

"Something up?"

She smiled at the sound of Xev's voice over the speaker. Until then, she'd forgotten how much she'd missed all of them.

"Yeah." Caleb scanned her body with a smirk. "Little bit of something just came in. I think you're going to want to see this for yourself."

"Is it important?"

"Probably more important than what you're currently doing, Grandpa. So stop licking your butt and get over here."

Kody bit her lip at Caleb's reference to the fact that Xev usually watched Nick while Xev was in the body of a housecat.

"I hate you so much, Malphas."

"Mutual." Caleb hung up.

Kody tsked at him. "Is that any way to speak to your brother?"

"It's the only way to speak to my brother. Besides" — Caleb jerked his chin behind her— "he started it."

She turned to see Xev standing in the shadows behind her.

Her heart stopped as she saw him, and tears again stung her eyes. Even taller than Nick, he was a massive beast. With long black hair that reminded her of her uncle, Acheron, he had eyes like a kaleidoscope that was made up of blues and browns, and tinged with green.

No one had eyes like his.

He seized her in a fierce hug. "What are you doing here? You died!"

Kody reveled in the warmth of that embrace. Long ago, Xev had sacrificed everything for the ones he loved, and that heart showed in everything he did. "I came back to help all of you."

Caleb frowned. "Help us do what? It's been really calm here since Nick went back to being human."

She stepped away from Xev. "It won't be for long. We have to stop Cyprian. He continues to muck up the timeline and I'm sure he's still here." As their leader, the Malachai, Cyprian was the highest form of demon.

Born in the future, Cyprian had traveled back in time and killed Kody. His intent was clear— he wanted to alienate Nick from all his friends and turn him into an even scarier Malachai than he was destined to be.

The more power Nick had at the time of Cyprian's birth, the stronger Cyprian would be when he killed Nick and assumed his power. The sad part? Cyprian could only create that power one way.

Isolate Nick from his friends and family.

An impossible task unless Cyprian killed those friends and family.

Their loyalty was above reproach and couldn't be broken by any other means. Since he had all of Nick's memories, Cyprian knew that as well as they did.

So, they all exchanged nervous glances.

Xev narrowed his gaze on Kody. "What do you mean mucking up the timeline? Nick killed Cyprian for what he did to you."

True, and yet... "Nick didn't stop anything by killing him in *this* time period. Cyprian isn't dead." Because their past where Nick had killed him was Cyprian's future and, in the future, Nick was dead. Cyprian wasn't. There always had to be a living Malachai. That was their curse.

Kill one when there was no replacement for him, and that Malachai would return to life.

So unless they could save the future Nick from dying in battle, they couldn't kill Cyprian in this time period.

Nick could kill Cyprian a thousand times and Cyprian would bounce back to life in the future and be able to return to this time or any other and run amok with Nick's life.

Cyprian was currently invincible.

The Arelim had used the same exact ploy with Kody when she'd gone up against other Malachai in the past.

If the Malachai she was after killed her, they reanimated her to fight another Malachai, in another time period. The only reason the Arelim had left her dead after Cyprian had killed her was because they knew she'd fallen in love with Nick, and would never kill her future husband.

Not after she discovered the truth.

She'd made herself useless to their cause.

Which really made her mad given all the years they'd forced her into an awful cat-and-mouse game she'd never really wanted to participate in.

Now, she was tired of games. Tired of being used.

The only way they could stop the Cyprian Malachai was in his own time period. Not Nick's.

"We have to go forward in time before Cyprian travels back again to this or another point and destroys Nick's life."

Caleb screwed his face up. "*We* don't *have* to do anything. We could just ride this all out as we planned."

True. Still, Kody maintained her hope. "But you're going to help me, right?"

"How?" Xev asked her. "Nick currently has no memory of any of us, or what's happened over the last couple of years. We intentionally locked away all his memories to protect him and the timeline. For all he knows right now, he's just a human boy whose father died in prison."

A step they'd believed would keep Nick from altering time and his own future. If he didn't know about what nightmares were ahead for him, and thought himself a regular teenager, then he wouldn't mess up the events that needed to occur to turn him into the Malachai Kody would eventually marry.

Regardless of tragedy, they had to guard the timeline. That had been their priority.

Until Kody realized that Nick wasn't the villain.

Cyprian was.

And if they didn't repair all this, the world would fall to Cyprian's brutality.

Unlike the men around her, she had seen and lived that bitter future. It was a horror they had to stop at all costs.

Kody held up the vial she'd taken as soon as she'd left Artemis on Olympus. Before she'd returned to the human world. "I have water from Mnemosyne. We can make Nick remember everything we took from him."

Caleb looked less than convinced by her plan. "We make him remember, then what?"

"I see where she's going, mate." Aeron winked at her. "We get his brains back, then we finish what we started. Hunt down the wanker in the future and stop him from killing our Nick."

"*And us.* I like the *stop him from killing us* part even more." Vawn grinned. "Really. That's me favorite part."

"And keep Cyprian from turning evil," Kody added. "We might be able to save him, too."

Caleb rubbed at the pain that was starting to throb in his head, as her optimism irritated him.

Why did they always want to save the person they should be putting down with extreme prejudice? Might sound harsh, but he was a demon, after all. Killing was more natural to his way of thinking than saving someone.

"I think you're all insane." He shifted his gaze from Kody to Xev and the doom crew he still wasn't sure should have ever been reunited. "This is the dumbest idea any of you have come up with... and I've seen and barely survived some of the more stellar doozies y'all have concocted."

Xev scoffed at his words. "Well, supreme stellar stupidity has your name all over it, brother."

"I can't even with you right now, Xev. I can't." Caleb let out a long, disgusted sigh over an invitation he'd never wanted.

Kody stepped forward between them. "It's our only hope to save them both. We *have* to do this."

Caleb curled his lip. "Do I look like Obi-Wan Kenobi?"

Laughing, Aeron clapped him on the back. "C'mon, Demon Kenobi. Won't be the same without you. Think of the fun we'll have."

"Thinking more of the blood I'll lose. My neck. Feathers... sanity... not that that didn't wave bye-bye to me about the time I met the sorry lot of you all."

"It's for our own wee Nicky." Vawn just had to pile on. "You know you love the little tosser as much as we do. Maybe even a bit more. And it's a lot more fun when he's his old self than the lamb who has no idea who we are."

Caleb really, really wanted to deny them. He'd already bled enough in this war. Lost too much he cared about, and that was the problem.

He'd lost too much.

Like them, he didn't want to lose anyone else. Not even the giant pain known as Nick Gautier.

"Fine. But when they kill me, I will be around to haunt you all. And it won't be a fun Caspar haunt. It'll be gory and severe. Japanese-horror-level terror."

"So normal, then." Aeron laughed. "Our absolute happy wheelhouse. We'll make sure and put that on your tombstone, boyo."

1

NEW ORLEANS, AUGUST 2000

Nick sighed as he walked out of the classroom and into heat so searing and humid, it felt like he'd just stepped into a vat of hot soup. The air was thick and clung to the back of his throat with a vicious grip.

Why was New Orleans so miserable in the summer? He loved this city more than anything, but dang.

You think this is hot, boy, try walking in armor across a desert, carrying blistering gear that weighs more than your horse.

Yeah, he'd learned a long time ago not to complain to his Dark-Hunter boss, Kyrian, about the heat. Forget it was snowing uphill both ways...

Kyrian always trumped his misery with a story so horrible, Nick didn't even attempt to compare trauma.

"You're right, Lord and Tormentor. No one's cruci-
fying me." Literally. His immortal boss had been
executed by Romans after weeks of being tortured for
information.

Still...

It was hot and his books were heavy.

"Nick?"

He paused at the sound of a voice that seemed eerily
familiar. But as he narrowed his gaze on the girl
approaching him, he didn't recognize her at all. She was
a head shorter than him with dark, curly hair and skin
that glowed with youthful exuberance.

Dang, she was beautiful.

She stopped in front of him with an adorable grin.
"Can I borrow your notes from yesterday?"

"You're in my class?"

She nodded.

How on earth had he failed to see her? *Yeah, something's wrong with me.*

He'd been working too hard.

"Uh, sure." He stepped over to a bench to put his
backpack down so that he could dig his notebook out.

"Hot out, isn't it?"

"Yeah. I'm dying."

With another beguiling smile, she held a bottle of

water out toward him. "Here. I think you could use this more than me."

Nick hesitated. "You sure?"

"Yeah. I have another." She handed it to him, and then pulled that second bottle from her pink backpack.

Nick exchanged his notebook for the water, then popped the top. She took a sip as he guzzled his. Probably not the smoothest move, but he was dying of thirst.

But as he drank, his head started spinning. "What the..." He staggered back, trying to get his bearings.

The girl helped him to sit on the bench next to his backpack. "Just breathe."

Easier said than done. This was like the craziest teacup ride he'd ever had. The entire planet slanted and spun. He put his head between his knees.

Just when he couldn't take it anymore, something loud popped in his ears.

The world stopped moving.

And he knew the name of the girl standing beside him. "Kody?"

Tears filled her eyes as she nodded.

Rising, Nick grabbed her into a giant hug and held her like the unspeakably precious girl she was. His anchor. The one thing that kept him sane and calm.

But if she was here and his memories were restored...

"Ugh, God. What happened?" It had to be bad.

And he was right.

"You know, the world is on fire, and we have to stop the dreaded evil. I believe you used to call this Typical Tuesday."

That he did.

And as he looked past Kody, he saw the rest of his team. Xev. Caleb. Kaziel. Zavid. Vawn.

And Lucky Charms Legolas.

"Yeah, this has to be bad." They wouldn't restore his memories for no reason. When last they'd parted ways, he wasn't supposed to ever have them restored lest he interfere with the future.

Sometimes lack of knowledge was a good thing. Especially when that knowledge could seriously muck up the future and end the world.

Kody sighed. "It's as bad as you're thinking. Cyprian didn't die."

Nick went cold at those words. "What?"

"You didn't kill him, and he's still determined to end us all."

Well that just stunk...

When you killed a guy, the least he could do was stay dead. How rude and inconsiderate.

Yeah, he knew how sick a thought that was. And it

would bother him a lot more had Cyprian not murdered everyone Nick loved.

Worse? He'd blamed it on Nick.

Yeah, some people just couldn't be reasoned with or trusted to do the right thing.

A Malachai was one of them and he should know given that he was the current head demon in charge. But at least he had a heart and soul, thanks to his mother. In all the hundreds of thousands of years since the Malachai race had been cursed, Nick was the only one who hadn't been hated by his mother.

Raised on abuse.

His mother had broken the cycle and while the villains thought it made him weak, Nick knew the truth. His mother had given him an inner strength unlike anything any Malachai had ever known.

How could he be so sure? He held all the memories of every Malachai who'd come before him. It wasn't his ego speaking, it was the truth.

Unlike his forefathers, he had that rare peace that came with knowing he was loved. Knowing there was someone in the world who valued his life more than she valued her own.

Two such souls, if he counted Kody.

And he did. How could he not? She kept him calm

when nothing else worked. The touch of her hand soothed his blackened soul.

Which was why he had to protect her at all costs. "So, if we can't kill him, how to we stop him?"

Kody flashed an evil grin. "I have an idea. But I doubt you'll like it."

2

NEW ORLEANS, APRIL 3227

Ambrose scowled as he felt a strange presence in his study. It was intense and powerful. Unlike anything he'd experienced in a long, long time. It crawled over his skin. A whispered breath with legs. Insidious and compelling.

Immediately on high alert, he flashed himself into the room to confront whatever had dared to defy his sigils and invade his domain.

Whoever it was, they would regret this stupidity.

He'd make sure of it.

At least, that was his thought until he came face-to-face with the last thing he expected.

A snot-nosed young man who bore a frightening resemblance to himself. Right down to a tacky yellow Hawaiian shirt that all but glowed in the dark. Even now, he both cringed and was warmed by the memory of his mother's happiness whenever he'd worn one of those ghastly things that should have been set on fire. Preferably with him in it.

What the hell?

Even more shocking, the kid wasn't alone. Ambrose's demon companion Caleb was with him. Along with Aeron, Kaziel, Xev, Zavid, and Vawn, and a young woman he didn't recognize.

"What is this?"

The boy "Nick" stepped forward. "You're going to want to sit down, old man. After all, I got the idea from you. At least a future you, I hope." He grinned. "I'm the old you from the past, and I'm here so that we can fix the timeline *y'all* screwed up. And hopefully save the life of our son and everyone else we love."

Hallucination? That was the first thought in Ambrose's mind. How else to explain this?

Then again...

They were supernatural beings. Logic had no place here. And he'd think they were even crazier, except for one thing...

"Where's Takeshi?" Ambrose asked. He was one of the few beings who could bend time to his will and make this possible. More than that, Takeshi had been his friend for centuries. Ever since Ambrose had freed Takeshi's wife from service to the Malachai.

So, if someone was helping him to travel through time and break laws that could get them both in trouble... Takeshi was the first culprit who came to mind.

"Keeping his head low. Last thing he wants is to attract the notice of those who would take exception to his helping us do what they don't want done."

I.E. time travel.

Made sense. And that sounded like the muddled crap that had come out of his mouth when he was a boy. "Could you be any more confusing?"

"Of course, I can. *You* know I can. We usually take pride in being irritating. Lucky for you though, I don't have the time to waste to make that vein in your temple start throbbing." Young Nick laughed. "Tell us what you know so far. Have you gone back in time to try to alter the past?"

That aforementioned vein was starting to throb. "Since I have no idea what you're talking about, I'm going to say no."

Nick passed a relieved glance to Kody. "Good. We got to him in time."

Ambrose hated the sound of that. It actually made his stomach cramp. "In time for what?"

Aeron pulled back the closed curtain in Ambrose's

living room to show them a burned-out, desolate land-scape that had replaced the once bustling city he'd grown up in. "Stop Armageddon, by the looks of it."

Nick's jaw went slack as he moved forward to see the hollowed-out buildings and debris that lined his beloved Bourbon Street. It looked like a nightmare he'd once seen.

Or the landscape he'd visited during Cyprian's reign.

"What happened?" he asked Ambrose, breathlessly.

Ambrose shook his head bitterly as he used his powers to close the curtains and block the view he'd once cherished. "It began with rioting. Lawlessness. The police force quit or was fired. The preters were discovered, and mankind didn't take it well. They attacked us. Tried to control us. Tried to sanction us. Then the wars came... Finally, the old gods decided we'd screwed up the planet enough, and they stepped in with a war of their own. The Chthonians returned to try to protect everyone from the gods' anger. In the end, they started bickering again among themselves." He winced at the unwanted memories. "Now, they all continue to battle for control. Mankind, monsters, Chthonians and gods. This isn't a place to raise children, so I have no idea what you're talking about when you tell me we have a son. I wouldn't be so stupid or selfish as to bring new and especially innocent life into *this* world."

Kody sighed heavily. "What year is it?"

"3227."

"No kidding?" Nick gaped at the disclosure. That would make him over a thousand years old. He couldn't even begin to imagine living that long, and yet he was staring at his future self. While he'd known the Ambrose who came back to save them was old, this hit home in a way nothing else ever had.

All the changes that must have happened in the world.

All the nightmares he must have witnessed and lived through...

He regretted ever giving Ambrose an ounce of lip over anything, and now he held a whole new respect for his future and the man he'd one day become.

No wonder he'd violated time laws to try and stop this from happening. To watch as the world he knew had been torn asunder...

Wow.

Horrified, he met Kody's gaze.

She smiled sadly. "I was born in 3225."

That meant that she was currently alive in this time period...

As a toddler.

Nick screwed his face up, then slapped Ambrose's arm. "You perv! You married an infant?"

"What?" Ambrose asked, offended as he rubbed his biceps.

Kody rolled her eyes. "I was twenty-one when we first met, Nick. Not an infant. Physically, we're just a couple of years apart in age."

Physically they might appear around the same age.

But in reality...

Screwing his face up, Nick shook his head. "I'm so grossed out right now. I need a minute. I just can't wrap my head around this." He curled his lip. "I'm like an ancient, old nasty man when we meet! How was that possible? Ew!"

Offended, Ambrose arched a brow at that. "Physically, I'm twenty-four. Not much older than you are now."

With an irritated smirk, Kody crossed her arms over her chest. "Do you know how much older Acheron will be than his wife? Or Kyrian when he meets his?"

"Or how much older I was than my wife?" Caleb added. "Trust me, age loses all meaning when you live for centuries."

Nick curled his lip. "Yeah, but I'm a teenager. That's not the state of my head. Ew! You people are so nasty!"

But at least that explained why Ambrose had held no knowledge of Kody when Nick had first met him.

Ambrose hadn't met her before he came back in time to knock sense into Nick.

Which made Nick think of something else as he looked at Kody. "Doesn't this make you a cougar in my time period? You are how old again?"

Rolling her eyes, she repeated Caleb's earlier words. "I can't even with you right now, Nick. I can't." She sighed, then turned toward Ambrose. "Why did I ever fall in love with either of you?"

She held a hand, palm outward, toward Ambrose. "You frustrated me on so many levels. And you..." She glared at Nick. "Why? Why? Why? I will *never* understand what I saw in either one of you. My dad was right. I could have done so much better."

"What?"

"Pardon?"

They spoke simultaneously.

"Ah now, don't you even act offended. Either of you. And you don't want to know what Acheron said when I dragged your sorry butt home that first time."

Ambrose snorted. "That, I can only imagine as I know what he said to me other times. I swear I hear it in my head. Especially given what he said to my face."

"Yeah," Kody agreed. "His reaction was second only to when Simi came home with her boyfriend."

Ambrose let out a nervous laugh. "*That*, I am all too familiar with."

"I know you know." Kody shook her head. "I remember you filling me in on the details about how she'd met her husband, and what Uncle Uh-Oh did when she brought *him* home the first time."

Nick was confused. "Uncle Uh-Oh?"

She gave the most beautiful smile Nick had ever seen. "It's what I called Acheron when I was little. I couldn't quite say Ash or Acheron, so my dad taught me to call him Uncle Uh-Oh. More to aggravate him than to help me."

Another laugh rumbled out of Ambrose. "That sounds like Styxx. He's always picking at Ash in a way no one else dares... not even me."

Nick snorted. "That's because we never know when his love for us will end, and his PTSD is going to kick in and make him strangle us."

A dark light appeared in Ambrose's eyes.

Nick backed off, realizing he must have plucked some future memory Ambrose had that he was missing. Since he didn't want to do any more damage to the time-line, he left it alone, and didn't ask the question that was burning inside him.

What had happened?

That was for another day.

Right now, they had something much larger to deal with.

Nick sighed. "I guess we need to start comparing notes to see who knows what."

"What do you mean?" Ambrose asked.

"Well, you obviously didn't know you had a son. Given our curse, we know that Kody isn't the mother."

Ambrose didn't quite follow the logic. "How do you know that?"

Kody smirked. "I'd remember having a son. That's not something a woman forgets. Which means someone else has to be the mother."

Nick clicked his teeth. "So who you been getting frisky with, old man?"

Ambrose narrowed his gaze on all of them. "None of your businesses, boy, but I can guarantee you this— she's not the mother of any child of mine, nor will she be. And what I do with her will not create a Malachai."

Because a Malachai could only be conceived through an act of violence.

Created in violence to do violence.

Which made Nick think of something he'd never thought of before. "So, how do we have a brother who's a sleep god? Given the curse. I mean, Dad didn't dare attack a god, did he?"

"No. Even Adarian wasn't *that* stupid. She was a

goddess who infiltrated his sleep. She was trying to feed off his rage and pain when he turned it all on her. Even in his dreams, Adarian was a handful."

"And she didn't kill him?"

"It was a dream, Nick. She went seeking something she shouldn't have and reaped the consequences of a really bad decision."

Be careful what you wish for... you just might get it. His mother's favorite curse.

"I still don't understand how that works. How could she conceive our brother in his sleep?"

Caleb put his hands on his hips. "Easy. She was a goddess and dreams are her reality. So for her, it didn't matter if they were in the dream world or the real one. They are the same for her. Worse, she would have gotten into trouble for being in his dreams had anyone known about it. Sleep gods weren't supposed to be doing that, especially infiltrating the dreams of demons like your father. Besides, Adarian would have torn her apart had he found out it was real and not a dream, as he was doing his best *not* to have a son who would kill him as soon as that son came of age. She didn't dare tell anyone who Madoc's father was. Adarian would have killed her... or Zeus."

Given that Adarian had lived longer than any

Malachai before him, that made sense. He'd been known for eating any and all children he'd ever sired.

Even the girls, who, sexist as it was, could never become a Malachai. It was just a chance he wouldn't take. When it came to losing power or risking emotions, Adarian didn't play.

And that made Nick think of something else. "Then we're looking for a goddess."

Ambrose frowned. "What? How?"

"Think about it. If Madoc was born from a goddess, wouldn't Cyprian have to be the same? The son of someone who tricked us or preyed on us in our sleep?" That made the most sense.

Actually, it made the only sense.

"Could also be a demon," Xev reminded them. "A demon would have the same powers to infiltrate your dreams. At least some of them."

Aeron clapped Nick on the back. "Good job, boyo. You've narrowed it down to everything not human. I'll get started on that list right away. Should take me, what? Eight, nine thousand years?"

"Shut up!" Nick shoved him playfully.

"It is a start," Kody said. "We at least have some idea of what we're looking for. Not all demons can enter dreams."

Caleb sighed. "Except we can't protect our dreams or

protect Nick in his. How can we stop a demon from going after him when he's unconscious?"

Nick scoffed at the very thought. "I've seen this movie. It's easy. Don't sleep! Freddy can't do anything as long as I'm awake."

Xev screwed his face up. "And I've dealt with you when you have no sleep. You're ridiculous, paranoid, and silly beyond endurance. One of us will most likely kill you." He met Ambrose's gaze. "Maybe we could ask Madoc or one of the other dream gods to help..."

"No." Ambrose's tone brooked no argument. "I don't want anyone else inside my head. Sleeping or awake. I've had more than my share with those animals in my sleep. Keep them away from me."

Nick agreed. "Yeah. My mind is a mass of chaos. I don't want anyone knowing my guilty or not-guilty secrets. It's just too weird."

"But we do need to figure this out." Ambrose stepped back. "Let's get some food."

Vawn, Aeron, and Kaziel grinned like fools, as they were always starving.

Nick let out a relieved breath. "Glad someone else is footing the bill. Feeding them is like hosting Simi at a barbecue."

That was true.

Nick clapped Ambrose on the back. "And while

we're eating, you can catch us up on what destroyed the world."

Ambrose scoffed at that. "I told you. Easy answer. Humanity. Humanity destroyed the world."

CYPRIAN MALACHAI HAD NEVER BEEN a creature of tolerance. Or one of patience. He'd learned cruelty from his mother's brutal fists and had never cared for much of anything.

Other than ending his father's life and assuming his powers. That was all he wanted.

All that mattered.

He had no real reason to destroy the world, other than he couldn't stand to see so many people happy while he'd never known anything other than hatred and bitterness. Why should they have it better or easier than he did?

He was the Malachai. The strongest of the strong.

It wasn't right that they had something that had been stripped from him. He couldn't help how he'd been born. Couldn't help being the hated Malachai.

Being cursed.

Why did they deserve love when he had nothing? When he had no one?

No, it was his job to right the scales. To make the entire world as hate-filled and bitter as he was. To see everyone suffer just as much as he did.

It was only right and fair that they suffered, too. Why should they inherit a world of happiness and safety, given the horrors of his past?

After his mother had tricked his father, he'd been born into a world of conflict and intolerance. That place had fed the beast inside him. Malachais sought out pain. It fed their powers and made them all the stronger.

That alone gave him pleasure. And made him want to make everyone around him endure utmost agony. The more they did, the better he felt. After all, misery loved company, and the larger the Brotherhood of Misery, the better. It was the only way he could have relief from the horrors of his existence.

That was the reason why he wanted to tear the world down and watch it all burn. To end his own pain with it.

There was just one problem...

"Where are they?" he growled.

"Pardon, my lord?"

He ignored his flunky demon. There were so many that he'd never bothered to learn their names, nor did he bother to pay them any attention.

What was the point? If he killed one, three more popped up, eager for his abuse.

I really need a hobby.

Other than pulling the wings off sentient creatures. But there was something satisfactory about the way they shrieked and begged for a mercy he completely lacked.

I am sick. At least he knew and understood it and willfully admitted he was a monster. But that changed nothing.

Frustrated, he teleported to the dark, dank dungeon where he kept the creature who'd begun this torture. Not with him...

With his ancestors.

Lilith.

She'd been sired when Chaos and Order had spun together for the very first time and joined to make life out of nothing. Or rather, the friction of their energies had formed the egg that birthed her and her siblings.

Legends claimed that the north wind had carried that very egg and set it down gently upon the earth to keep it from shattering and killing the seven gods inside.

When their egg had landed, light had sprung out through the darkness, cracking the egg in two. The bright blue goddess, Shyamala, known as the Queen of All Shadows, had emerged first. Apollymi, Acheron's mother, had been born second. Third to step out was

Cam, who would later be known as Nick's Aunt Menyara, or Mennie as he liked to call her. Her "birth" was followed by Rezar, Jaden, and Lilith. Kadar, Cyprian's maternal grandfather, who was also known as the King of All Darkness, had emerged last from the egg. It was why Kadar went by Noir. He was the eternal night to balance out his siblings.

Three born of order. Three of chaos.

Three of light. Three of dark.

One neutral spirit, Lilith.

It was said that when Lilith went to step out of their egg, she was either pushed by Kadar (a very likely scenario given his grandfather's venom) or that she slipped on a piece of the shell. For reasons unknown, that fall caused her powers to mix in a most unusual way.

In the beginning, unlike her brothers and sisters who had clearly been born of light or dark powers, she'd been neutral. Willful. Then time had marched on, changing her and her siblings.

Life had turned her so vengeful that she'd become a horrid creature, avoided by all. One who had no problem cursing Cyprian's entire line into oblivion for no reason other than they'd been born. Cursing them to this hated existence. For the sole surviving Malachai to be as cold and unloved as she was. Because she'd been preyed upon and cursed, Lilith felt justified doing that to others.

Even those who didn't deserve it.

It was why his great ancestor had captured her. So that all Malachai would be able to ensure that she never harmed anyone else. That she would be just as hated as they were.

For eternity.

Now, she stood frozen. Aware of everything and unable to affect anything.

A fate worse than death.

But still not as awful as she deserved for the curse she'd placed on them all. To know no love. To feel only hate. To never find peace or happiness. She was the sole reason he felt toward the world the way he did.

He paid forward her own disdain and continued her path of annihilation.

For every life she'd destroyed and all the hate she'd spread, there should be a more fitting punishment for her crimes.

But the only problem was that with all their abilities, no Malachai had ever thought of anything worse for Lilith. In spite of their combined malfeasance, this was the best his ancestors had devised.

Were the Malachai that impotent or just that unimaginative?

Of course, Cyprian was the only Malachai to ever think that about them. And he knew it for a fact, as he carried the memories of every Malachai who'd ever been born before him.

Sadly, the knowledge he wanted most, he didn't have.

Would anyone ever defeat him?

What son would he father to ultimately rise up and destroy him?

While they might live for centuries, no Malachai lived forever.

That, too, was their curse.

"I hate you," he snarled at her, knowing he wasn't the first to confront her.

Another part of their curse was that all Malachai walked the road of his predecessors.

Except for Cyprian's father. Nick Gautier had known love. Had been protected. By both his mother and the Adarian Malachai who'd sacrificed himself for his son.

Unprecedented throughout their history.

"And that's why I have to destroy you."

He wanted his father to know his pain and that of all their forefathers. To rise to his demon form like all those before them. Salivating for power and at the expense of his father's life.

Not helping to protect the humans who'd betrayed them. Helping the gods who'd damned them.

For those crimes alone, Nick Gautier had to die.

"How do I stop this?"

Lilith stared, unblinking. Her beautiful face was frozen and utter stone. Like his heart.

"Ugh. Here again, moping?"

He ground his teeth at the sound of his mother's disgust. "Don't you have someone else to torment?"

Arms crossed, she pranced forward. "I do. Which is why I resent having to seek you out. Especially since you're in the throes of another moody fit. Useless. From the moment you drew your first breath, until your last."

Fury whipped through him. "How dare you!"

She actually laughed in his face. "Really? That's your best threat? Don't think for one moment that I fear *you*."

Her disdain caused the Malachai to possess him. Change him into his winged demonic form. "I have crushed greater gods than you!"

"And I've plucked the eyes off many a Malachai and used them to feed my pets."

He would deny that, but she actually was that sick. There were times when having the memories of others was extremely inconvenient.

This was definitely one of them.

So as much as he hated it, he backed down. "What

brings you here, Mother? Other than the sick delight you take from mocking me?"

"My spy has told me that there's been a timeline spike."

His father.

"Where?"

"A year before you were born."

That didn't make any sense. While he'd assumed Caleb and the others would rally around his father, he didn't think it would be in *his* past. "I don't understand."

"Neither do I. Unless they're trying to stop you from being conceived, it makes no sense."

And they could never stop his conception. The only ones who knew the truth about it were his mother... and him. All others had been killed to ensure utter secrecy.

That was their way.

Trust no one. Kill anyone who might betray. Better to strike first than risk exposure.

It was the *only* way.

"How do we get to them?"

His mother snorted. "You don't just get in a car and drive there. You know how hard it was to reach them the last time."

Yeah. Time travel sucked. It'd left him sick and weak for days. So much so that he'd feared ever recovering.

The same was true about life. It wasn't for the meek

or cowardly. Some days it took all courage just to take another breath.

Another step.

"So what's the plan?"

She always had one. Being the original goddess of War, battle strategies were second nature to her. While he was good, she was the absolute best.

So even though it galled him to ask for her help, it was the smart thing to do.

One corner of her lips curled. "Kill them."

Of course. Her answer for everything. His, too, for that matter.

"Anything more concrete? Such as how to locate them so that we can slide a blade into their ribs or hearts?"

"We've pinpointed the time. You know the location."

The year before he was born. Yeah, he knew where his father would be. "Well that's just great, isn't it?"

At that time, his father had spent most of his time with Aunt Artie. On Mount Olympus. Bad thing about gods— they didn't like people intruding in their divine palaces. If he went to drag his father and crew out of Greece, Artemis would blast them to oblivion.

And while he was strong, they had to tread carefully around gods. Especially Artemis, who retained some of the powers she'd siphoned from Acheron.

Such as being a god killer.

Or more to the point, Malachai killer.

Given that she'd been feeding from Cyprian's father for years, she also shared Malachai powers... and unlike his father, her powers wouldn't diminish in his presence. Artemis would retain all those superior powers she'd collected.

And be able to use them against him.

Yeah, she wasn't one they wanted to confront, especially the year before his birth. The year Artemis would be at her strongest.

Not to mention, he knew he had never attacked his father at that time...

Keeper of memories. He knew his father's life. At least most of it.

"Again, I ask you if you have a plan, Mother?"

"Of course, I do. And this time, we will finish them and leave the door open for you to destroy mankind and to reign for eternity as the last Malachai."

3

Nick pulled the Eye of Ananke from his pocket. When his friends had taken his memory from him, he'd forgotten that he had this.

More importantly, he'd forgotten where he'd hidden it.

Like a fool, the moment his memory returned, he'd sought it out. There was just something about it that lured him.

A siren's curse.

"Oh my God!" Kody gasped as she entered the room and saw it in his hand. "I thought *that* was gone! For good!"

That was what he'd told her, that it was gone forever,

but... "I know it made me crazy. Still, I can't stop thinking about what Ambrose said."

"What did I say?"

He snorted as the older version of himself joined them in the sitting room. "To use it to reset all the things you changed. You regretted coming to the past and messing up so much of our life."

"So your answer was to come to the future and screw that up?"

Yeah, maybe this wasn't the best idea. "Didn't know what else to do. I figured the future me had to be smarter than the teenage me." At least, that was what he hoped.

Otherwise, they really were screwed.

Besides, the bleak future the stone had shown him was nothing as bad as Ambrose's current reality.

"I wanted to understand what I was fighting for."

"You know what you're fighting for." Ambrose gestured at the wall on Nick's left. A screen flickered on to show him a newscast.

Mesmerized, Nick couldn't take his gaze off the grisly sight. Being a New Orleans native, he was used to bad news reports. They seemed more the norm than happy events.

But this...

There were riots and battles everywhere. It looked as

if someone had detonated a nuke in the center of the city. Cars were overturned and burned out. Stones were missing. Buildings crumbling, with barbed wire wrapped around businesses and gates.

Tears welled up in his eyes at the destruction of a home that had meant everything to him, but he refused to let those tears fall. Instead, he held the pain inside and wished he'd never seen the horror of his future.

"Was it this bad the first time you came to see me?"

Ambrose shrugged. "Since I haven't done that yet, I have no idea what motivated me to seek you. My guess is it must not have improved."

"It could be the fact that we came here first." Kody jerked her chin at the Eye. "That would make sense, right?"

Ambrose nodded. "Especially if we're keeping time straight and I was only doing what I was so supposed to." He picked up the stone and grimaced. "I remember how much I hated this thing. It drove me crazy. Seeing all futures at once. Feeling the life force of the universe flowing in my veins and haunting my sleep."

"Exactly." Nick sighed. "I kind of hate you for giving it to me."

Kody didn't comment on that as she moved to stand beside Ambrose. "Where did you get it from?"

Ambrose turned it over in his hand. "An asshole who

wanted me to understand Savitar and Acheron gave it to me."

That wasn't helpful, as Nick knew a large number of assholes he'd had to deal with. "And which one might that be?"

"Thorn. He told me to use it to do the right thing. In retrospect, I'm thinking the right thing would have been to use this to bash him in the head."

Nick cringed as Ambrose mentioned the Prince of All Darkness. Thorn was an interesting character who walked a weird line between good and evil— which was why he traveled in their company.

Only thing about Thorn— he could be quite merciless if you rubbed him the wrong way. "You must have really hated me to hand it off in my direction, then."

"I do. Self-loathing is second nature to me. The more time passed, the worse it became."

Nick sighed as he considered what Ambrose had told him. "I still don't understand something."

"You're doing better than I am. There are lots of things I don't understand."

He ignored Ambrose's comment. "How is it that while I was working for Kyrian, we have no memory of *you* or this?" he asked, indicating the Eye.

"How do you know that?"

"You told me so."

Ambrose stroked the Dark-Hunter double bow mark that rested on his cheek. An unfortunate "gift" from Artemis when she brought him back to life after their mother had died. "A higher power must have intervened to take those memories."

"Any idea who?"

Kody shook her head. "Not Acheron. He'd never, ever do such a thing."

Nick agreed with Kody. Given the horrors of Acheron's life because someone had tried to circumvent his fate and his twin brother's, Acheron refused to tamper with anyone else's.

"We know it wasn't Savitar," Ambrose added.

Again, Nick agreed. When it came to interfering with fate, Savitar made Acheron look like a three-year-old with no impulse control. Like Acheron, Savitar would definitely never tamper with anyone's destiny.

A loud crash sounded.

Nick and Kody jumped, but Ambrose didn't even blink.

"What was that?" Nick asked.

Ambrose sighed heavily. "Demons at the gate. They hit my shields constantly and explode."

Nick was aghast. "And you let them?"

"Can't stop them. Barely tolerate them. The fact they want to commit suicide by dive-bombing my shields...

none of my business. It just goes to show how stupid they are and makes my cleaning bill ridiculous. Besides, it's a public service. They will now do no harm."

Ambrose meant that. There was no emotion whatsoever. In all honesty, Nick didn't like this version of himself.

How can I be so cold? His future self scared him. Because right now, the thought of someone, even a demon, dying like that saddened him and made him want to talk it over so that they could find a peaceful solution other than baked-on demon.

What happened to turn me into Ambrose?

Ambrose gave him a cold stare. *Talk to me after a demon murders our mother. What can I say? It left a lingering scar.*

Yeah, that'd do it. Before he had Kody to anchor him to humanity, he'd had his mother. She alone had kept his evil at bay and made him want to be someone she wouldn't be ashamed of. Without her or Kody around to inspire him, he had no reason not to end the world.

Honestly, he couldn't imagine a life without them, and Ambrose had lived centuries with no anchor. Centuries after the death of Cherise Gautier.

With only anger and bitterness. Memories he didn't want. Given what his mother meant to him, Nick could only imagine how insane her death would make him.

Nick slid a glance to Ambrose. *That answered that.*

And it was another reason he was here. "Can we save her?"

Ambrose shrugged. "I don't know. I've gone round and round with every possible scenario until I've made myself insane. If we save her, I won't become a Dark-Hunter or the Malachai."

"Would that be so bad? Then we wouldn't have Cyprian to deal with. If we really want to stop this brutal cycle, wouldn't saving my mother be a good idea?"

Ambrose sighed. "You change one thing, Nick, and there's no telling what could happen. The curse could bring Adarian back for all we know, and we don't know what he'd have done had he continued living... He could have formed a pack with gallu demons. Kept the Daimons from being able to walk in daylight. Or kill *us* — remember our history. Either the son kills the father, or the father kills the son. Adarian wanted Cherise. He kept us alive because he knew our death would be more than she could bear, and he didn't want to cause her pain. But the day might have come where he no longer cared about that, and sent Caleb or another out to murder you."

That would have destroyed his mother.

"Exactly. And there's no telling what Mom would have done. Killed herself or gone after him. The one thing we know about our mother... She lived for us. If we'd died..."

He was right. She would have self-destructed worse than they had.

Anything happens to you, Boo, they'll have to dig two graves. I will not live in this world if you're not here with me. She'd spoken those words to him so often and with such passion that they were an indelible imprint on his soul.

"You might never meet me," Kody reminded him. "Our daughter would never be born."

"We wouldn't have saved Acheron's wife, either."

Because he wouldn't have been working with Acheron's enemies.

Nick winced at the future events he'd seen. "I did so many inexcusable things... like help put Tory in danger."

Ambrose snorted. "But in the end, you made it right. And all the bad things we did, we did after our powers ignited."

Back when they couldn't control their anger. Because that was the very nature of a Malachai.

Destroy *everything*.

Ambrose stepped forward with a stern frown. "What all have you seen in that Eye?"

"A lot of things." Horrible things Nick wanted to avoid and forget. "Why?"

"Did you see us on Savitar's island?"

Nick wanted to deny it, but yeah. He'd seen that, too. After his mother was killed, he'd gone to war against Acheron. Unable to train him because of Nick's unreasoning hatred and blame, Acheron had sent him to Savitar for protection and training.

Nick could never get the sight of his future out of his mind. "Yeah, I saw it."

"Did you see why?"

"I was mad at Acheron."

Ambrose shook his head. "Acheron felt the Malachai in us. He knew exactly who and what we were, and what we were capable of, especially given our rage at that time. We were sent to Savitar to calm us down and delay the explosion of our powers. Savitar was supposed to help us channel our hatred and control the rage."

That made sense, given the serene environment Savitar lived in— a breathtaking vanishing isle that popped up on Earth wherever there was good surfing. But Sav and Ash had greatly underestimated the rage in Nick's heart.

For years, Nick/Ambrose hadn't understood why Savitar had taken him in, especially since Savitar hated intruders or any semblance of the "modern" world. The surly Chthonian much preferred complete and utter isolation away from everything and everyone.

Yet for reasons he'd refused to explain, Savitar had made an exception to help out Acheron.

No one understood why.

"Hey, boyo?"

Nick glanced at Aeron as he joined them. "Yeah?"

"Wanted to let you know, them demons aren't just hitting the wall. They're breaking through it, man."

"What!" Ambrose shot to his feet, then teleported from the room.

Confused, Nick had no idea where Ambrose had gone. He looked at Aeron. "Where are they?"

Motioning for Nick to follow, Aeron walked backward for two steps, then turned to rush down a posh hallway.

Nick followed fast until he came to one section of the house he recognized from the future events he'd glimpsed in the Eye.

The room where he'd found his mother murdered. Ambrose had never changed it from the days when their mother had decorated it. All his mother's favorite romance novels were still lined up in the cozy reading nook where she used to sit and read for hours on end. Even now, he could see her there, reading while she snacked on chips or crackers and sipped her Diet Coke.

It'd been the one future memory that he kept

returning to. A moment where his mother had seemed so happy and content.

So beautiful.

"Nick?" Kody touched his arm. "You okay, Boo?"

Tears choked him as he nodded. But it was a lie. He wasn't okay with any part of his future. Especially the part where he lost his mom.

It wasn't supposed to end like this.

All his life, he'd been told about karma. *What you sow, you shall reap.*

Yet it was far more often *sow the wind and reap the whirlwind.* Utter chaos.

His mother had never sown the discord and nightmares of her life. She'd been a good and decent woman who had struggled and worked hard in spite of all the agony and obstacles life had hurled at her.

Instead of giving him up for adoption so that she'd have a decent life, she'd raised him by herself. Made him a man she could be proud of instead of the demon he'd been born to become. No one deserved the misery of her life, and they damn sure didn't deserve the end life had given her.

Same for him. He'd done his best to be a good son. A good man. To do honor to his mother and what she'd taught him.

How had they been rewarded? His mother had died a horrible death. Alone.

Crying for help that never came.

Because of him. He'd been helping strangers that night. Not protecting his mother as he should have been.

The injustice burned inside him until he was sure every fiber of his being was screaming out for Artemis to come, take his soul, and help him claim vengeance on the ones who'd taken her life.

Screw karma. It was a sick lie peddled by those who wanted to make sense of a world that had none whatsoever. This wasn't justice.

Bad things just happened. For no reason whatsoever, and to good people as well as bad. *He maketh His sun to rise on the evil and on the good, and sendeth rain on the just and on the unjust.* One of his mother's favorite quotes to explain the misery that always seemed to hunt her down.

And that reminded him of something Acheron had once said to him. *"Deserving's got nothing to do with it, Nick. Life is always going to try you, and it's not going to stop as long as you have breath in your lungs. You can't tell anything about someone when everything's going their way. The real mettle of a person shows when everything's going wrong, and especially when they're suffering. You either lie down and let life run you over, or you get up and flip it off. Not today, bitches. You're not going to defeat me. I won't let you."*

But it was hard to stand up when you'd been kicked down your entire life.

And right now, they had demons demanding his head.

Pushing that pain away so that he could focus, Nick followed the others to the back, where the solarium allowed them to see the demons that were attacking the shield.

Ambrose took one look at them and sneered. "Really?" he shouted. Then he blasted them with more power than Nick had ever seen.

The demons screamed in agony before they burst apart and rained down a foul mess he hoped Ambrose didn't force him to clean.

Aeron, Vawn, and Kaziel gasped in unison.

Vawn grabbed Aeron's arm. "I don't want to burst into flames, man."

Ambrose glanced at Vawn over his shoulder. "Then don't piss me off."

Xev smacked his lips. "From one who has done that, I will say Ambrose isn't as mean as his father. Adarian was without a doubt one of the worst psycho Malachais ever born."

"Says the one who's been in service to them since the beginning."

Xev nodded at Caleb's comment. "None of them were tolerable... until Ambrose. He's a lot more forgiving, even when pissed. I would simply suggest you stay away from his shields."

Caleb turned away from the demon barbecue mess over their heads to face Ambrose. "So where exactly are our future selves... in this time period?"

Ambrose gave them a snide smirk. "You know where Nick is." He indicated himself, then jerked his chin at Kody. "She's in grade school."

"Stop!" Nick put his fingers in his ears. "You keep grossing me out with that. I don't know who the bigger perv is at this point. You for dating her in our future, or her for being an old woman who came back to date me in our past. Either way, it screws with my head."

Ambrose ignored him and his tirade. "The zoo crew —" he indicated Aeron, Vawn, and Kaziel— "went back to the UK with Zavid. Been a long time since I've heard anything from them, but when last we spoke, they were living it up and having a great time. Caleb is still in my service, as is Xev, but I refuse to tell you any more about them, as I don't want to screw up history."

Nick agreed. He knew exactly why Ambrose wasn't telling them their futures.

"Same with Simi." Ambrose turned toward Kody. "You know what happens, right?"

"As long as it doesn't change. I know what they were doing when I was a child and after Nick and I started dating. I assume they're living the same lives they had before."

Ambrose inclined his head. "That's our goal, then. Preserve the timeline."

"How do we do that?"

Caleb snorted. "Erase Nick's memory and put him back at home."

"We tried that," Xev reminded him. "And they kept coming for him."

"Because of Cyprian." Kody sighed as she met Ambrose's gaze. "You have no memory of him, correct?"

"None."

"Then he wasn't here before. You ran across him in high school, but not at any other future time... until you two battled and he killed you."

Nick placed the heels of his hands against his eyes. "This makes my head hurt."

Aeron clapped him on the back. "Time travel always does that, laddie. It's why most creatures don't tamper with it. Not worth the migraine."

Nick shook his head. "But Were-Hunters do, right?

They don't live chronologically. How do they not damage lives when they pop back and forth?"

"Most of them don't hop around," Ambrose answered. "They pick a time and live there. Usually in isolation from the rest of the world so that they don't cause problems or change things. They only hop when they're being chased and they're trying to find some place safe for their families."

That made sense, and Nick remembered the Bear clan in New Orleans talking about it. They had only time jumped a handful of times before settling in New Orleans. Once there, they'd founded Sanctuary, the bar and grill where all preternatural beings were welcomed and protected.

Even so, he couldn't shake the sensation that this was new ground, not something that was destined. "I feel like everything is out of control."

Kody sighed. "I feel like I'm the one who started this. If I hadn't been so filled with rage thinking the Ambrose Malachai had murdered my family, I would never have agreed to go back and destroy Nick."

Xev scratched his chin. "That's assuming you didn't do that originally."

Ambrose shook his head. "Had she been there originally, I would have a memory of it by now."

"Would you?" Caleb asked.

Ambrose paused as he considered that. Time laws were peculiar things, and to be honest, he wasn't an expert in them. Since Malachais didn't time travel, he'd never paid much attention to the creatures who had those powers.

Or the rules of time travel. Other than the main one — never, *ever* do it.

But he was sure about one thing. "I have the memories of all Malachai. Even if my memories had been bound, they would have been freed when my powers took over."

"That makes sense." Kody rubbed Nick's back. "Sadly, the only person who can really tell us what memories are what is Cyprian."

"Wait a minute..." Xev's face lost all color. "Inheritance. Think about it... Cyprian went back in time. Malachais can't do that. If he time traveled, it means he must have inherited those powers from his mother. Right?"

Ambrose felt his own color fade from his face. "You're right. She'd have to have them for him to inherit."

"Would she?" Nick asked. "We time traveled here, and you traveled to my time even though we don't have the powers. Couldn't he have hitchhiked those powers the same way we did?"

"He could, but that would leave a trail. Just like we both leave one for our enemies to follow." Ambrose stroked his chin as he considered the matter. "The fact he leaves no mark means the powers come from within him and not a secondary source. Besides, no preternatural creature would be so stupid as to help a Malachai travel back in time to increase his powers. Most crap the bed whenever our name is mentioned." Ambrose met Nick's gaze. "Since we both know that we'd never attack a woman and would never be attacked by one, that means Cyprian's mother is either a demon or a goddess who can walk in dreams and attack us there. It's the only thing that makes sense and it's the only way he could have been born."

Caleb started pacing. "So, we're looking for a woman who can infiltrate dreams *and* walk through time."

Ambrose nodded at Caleb. "We're definitely looking for a Skoti."

Kody shook her head. "But they disbanded, right? Once Zeus's curse was broken, I thought the Skoti stopped siphoning emotions from humans. There's no need now that they have their own feelings restored."

"Not all of them stopped preying on humans." Ambrose paused as he thought about the matter. "Emotions are an addiction, and after..." He paused again as he almost disclosed facts they didn't know about their future.

That could be disastrous.

"After a certain couple of events Nick and everyone but Kody will live through, some of them remained on the dark side."

"What about our half-brother Madoc?" Nick asked. "Which side did he choose?"

Ambrose gave him a wry grin. "Believe it or not, he was untouched by being Adarian's son. Our brother has no Malachai tendencies or desires. No idea how *that* happened. Maybe a byproduct of having his emotions drained for so long or because he's part god. Either way, he's never been controlled by his baser emotions."

"Lucky him." Nick let out a tired sigh. "Then could he help us narrow this down to who or what we're looking for?"

"We can try."

Caleb cleared his throat to get Ambrose's attention. "We—" he indicated Xev and the rest— "Aren't exactly welcomed around other gods and definitely not on Mount Olympus. How about we wait here for your return?"

Ambrose inclined his head at that sound logic. Given the fact that the other gods viewed them as parasites and traitors— or worse, enemies— that made a lot of sense. "Keep the gutter demons out of my house and don't touch anything until we get back."

Caleb smirked. "I'll just save them for you to deal with on your return."

"One thing." Xev took a step toward Ambrose. "What do we do if our future selves show up?"

Ambrose snorted dismissively. "You won't. Y'all only bug me when I call for you. And you always text first."

"Good to know." Xev stepped back toward Caleb. "We are *not* watching porn."

Caleb screwed his face up. "I don't watch porn."

"What do you call that weird anime you're addicted to?"

"Anime. I don't watch hentai."

"I don't see a difference."

"Well, I'd show you the difference, but I don't watch hentai."

Ambrose covered his ears. "God, I forgot how frustrating it was when all y'all got together."

Nick tsked. "Now, now, *grand-père*, they just gonna pass a good time. What say we slide on out of here and chase the *grande fifolet, n'est pas*?"

Ambrose gave him a stern glower. "Don't even try that with me, *Bouki*. I'm the one person who won't fall for your Cajun charm. And we're not chasing a ghost light. We're about to aggravate a god I'd rather not bother. While we're not on bad terms, we're not exactly friends, either. Madoc keeps to his space and I keep to mine."

Kody wrapped her arm around Nick's. "I'm coming, too."

Ambrose started to argue, but she, unlike the others, shouldn't aggravate Madoc simply by being in his presence. While her mother was a goddess and her father a Chthonian, they were well respected by all pantheons. "Fine."

He teleported them to the Hall of Mirrors on the Vanishing Isle just outside of Olympus. This was where the Dream-Hunters still made their divine home far away from the human world.

Nick stumbled as he looked around a place he'd only heard about. It was a regal hall that reflected hundreds, if not thousands, of portals. Portals that led not only to the world of man and other dimensions, but also to the dreams of unprotected humans.

Back in the day, the sleep gods had used these portals to prey on hapless humans just so that they could feel some sort of emotion, as Zeus had banned all emotions from them after one of their brethren had played a prank on him. The king of the Greek gods wasn't exactly known for his sense of humor.

Rather for his vindictive nature.

Instead of just punishing the lone idiot who'd tricked him, he'd gone after every one of the sleep gods to ensure none of them ever decided to play a trick again.

"Shouldn't Madoc be here?" Nick asked.

Ambrose shook his head. "He'll be in the Onethalamus."

There was one of those words Nick hated. "The who-what?"

"Their meeting hall. Once word reaches him, and I'm sure he's already been told that someone arrived through the portal, he'll be there to greet us. They're not exactly thrilled with unannounced visitors."

Nick hesitated at one important word. "They?"

"Delphine, Zeth, and Madoc. The Dream-Hunter High Council."

"Ah." It was good to know who was in charge.

The Dream-Hunters had been created centuries ago to go after the Skoti who preyed on sleeping humans. Skoti were the nasty consequence of Zeus having stripped the dream gods of their emotions. Since they couldn't feel anything in their normal existence, some of them had discovered that if they entered human sleep, they could siphon emotions off the dreaming humans.

The bad thing about siphoning emotions was that it became addictive. And the stronger the emotion, the more buzz the god received. As a result, some of them became dream predators who latched on to humans who had volatile dreams so much that it invariably drove the human insane.

And often to suicide.

To prevent those Skoti from harming unsuspecting humans, Dream-Hunters had been created as a type of dream police. Their job was to stop the Skoti before Zeus found out and punished all of them for daring to try and circumvent his curse.

Too bad the Dream-Hunters had missed the succubus who'd abused Nick/Ambrose so that she could conceive Cyprian.

When seconds count, the police are only an hour away.

That old joke seriously haunted him now.

Nick passed a glance to Kody before he met Ambrose's gaze. "When did we meet the council?"

Ambrose shrugged. "A long time ago for me. Not too far in your future."

Nick scoffed. That settled nothing.

But he could tell that his future self was getting aggravated, so he followed Ambrose down a brightly lit marble hallway unlike anything he'd ever seen before. It was so bright, it reminded him of standing on a beach with the sun directly overhead. Really, he should have brought sunglasses. He couldn't imagine how Ambrose stood it, given he had the light-sensitive eyes of a Dark-Hunter. It had to be excruciating for him.

There was only one door for them to enter. Ambrose opened it and allowed him and Kody to go in first.

Nick drew up short as he saw a man who was actually taller than them. Rare to find, given that at almost six and a half feet tall, they towered over most people.

In his opinion, their brother looked nothing like them. Whereas Ambrose was muscular, Madoc was lean, with long black hair and eyes so blue, they appeared to glow. While Nick still had his blue eyes, they were nowhere near the same shade.

Ambrose had the black eyes of a Dark-Hunter.

Madoc's stern expression softened as he saw Ambrose enter behind them, and he stepped forward. "Is this Nick? As in you as a boy, Nick?" he asked Ambrose.

Ambrose nodded. "He just showed up on my doorstep."

"How?"

"Takeshi."

Madoc frowned at the answer. "I should have said, why?"

"I'm sure you know." Ambrose rolled his eyes in Nick's direction. "He tends to know everything. It's his most annoying habit."

Madoc's stare turned irritated before a strange, faraway light filled his eyes. His frown turned darker, more pronounced. "It's odd how fate works, isn't it? I should have been you instead of you, but the Malachai never rose up within me."

Ambrose snorted. "Be glad. It's what saved your life."

"No. The fact that Adarian had no idea I existed and I never let him know of my existence is what saved my life." Madoc glanced at Nick. "When a Malachai son is born, the Malachai father always knows. You can't keep it from them."

"You sure about that?" Ambrose asked. "Dad didn't seem to know about you."

"Because I was in another realm with my emotions completely bound, and my goddess mother shielding me and my abilities out of fear of what he might do to her if he found out I existed. There was no way for him to know about me."

That made sense to Nick. "You being a god saved you."

"It might have saved me, but my fear is that it's most likely what caused *your* mother to die."

Nick's stomach sank. "Pardon?"

Madoc's gaze turned dark, his features strained. "At the time your mother was killed, the curse against my kind was breaking."

"A major crossroad," Ambrose breathed. "The two Malachai bloodlines converged."

Madoc nodded. "Had you died at that time, and it's the one and only time you *could* have died, I would have become the Malachai in your place."

Ambrose sucked his breath in sharply. "What are you saying?"

"With my god powers, the uncontrollable rage I had then, and the army of Dream-Hunters I commanded... That would have been enough. But when you combine all that with the demons and furious Skoti wanting revenge..."

"We'd all be dead," Kody finished.

"Yes, you would."

Kody bit her lip. "Could you become a Malachai now?"

"In theory, maybe, but I really don't have the hate and anger for it anymore. That righteous fury inside me came and went rather quickly."

Kody glanced at Nick, then Ambrose. "So what would happen if Nick or Ambrose died and there was no one to replace them?"

An evil dimple appeared in Ambrose's cheek. "We can't. There always has to be one Malachai. It's part of our punishment."

Madoc nodded. "When Nick died, I could have

emerged as another Malachai."

"But I went to Artemis to extract my revenge on the one who killed my mother." Ambrose winced.

"Yes, and you saved the world by doing that. Again, had I inherited the powers at that point in time, I would have been unstoppable, and I would never have had a child to curtail my powers— or anyone else who could have contained me."

Being a god, Madoc was the one and only being who could have circumvented the mortal part of their curse. So long as he had no son, and he could control that with his powers, Madoc would have lived on forever.

There would never have been a son to replace him, and he would have commanded omnipotent powers. Two massive armies to do his bidding. No one would have been able to defeat him.

Ever.

Not even Apollymi or Acheron.

Kody moved to stand next to Nick. "Are you sure? How do we know Nick wouldn't have come back regardless of Artemis's interference?"

Madoc shrugged. "You're right. We don't know for sure. It could have swung either way. I still might not have inherited the powers, and Nick might have come back to life on his own. Guess we'll never know the truth of that moment since Artemis was there and stepped in."

Ambrose sighed heavily. "We screwed up a lot, little brother."

"Because we were never told the truth." Anger ran through Nick as he realized how much damage had been done by those who'd bound his powers to keep him from exploding.

Like Acheron. Menyara. Savitar.

Had they just left him alone...

Madoc placed a comforting hand on his shoulder. "Think of it this way, Nick... when you died, someone, most likely Azura or Noir, was trying to put me in power. I'm not you, and I don't have any memories of a happy childhood or a loving mother. As a Malachai, I would have nothing to rein me in or make me sane. You and your mother made a sacrifice that saved the world. Malachai blood or not. Because I promise you, had that title come to me at that time when my rage against the gods was boiling over... I would have made Adarian look like an angry toddler."

In a weird way, that did make him feel better.

No, it didn't.

Stop it! You're being selfish. It was comforting to know that if his mother had to die, she'd saved the world in the process. It would have made Cherise Gautier proud, and she would gladly have volunteered her life to protect others.

Still, it hurt him to know that she was gone. Even if the reason was a good one.

I'm sorry, Mom.

He blinked back tears as he met Madoc's cold stare. "I can't save her, can I?"

"If you do, you have to figure out some way to keep me from going Skoti and Malachai at the same time. Trust me, little brother, you wouldn't have survived fighting me. While your powers wouldn't have been diminished in the confrontation, mine wouldn't have been weakened either."

That was scary to think about.

In fact, it reminded Nick of Godzilla going up against Mothra.

Still, he was trying to make sense of it all. "I'm so confused. We know what happens. How we all came to be here. And now that we know, can't we stop it?"

"This isn't a train schedule, Nick." Madoc held his hand up, and the room shimmered with a million images of fate playing out. It was eerily similar to the Eye, only not as confusing. "It's not the past you have to change... It's the future."

4

S cowling, Nick stared at Madoc. "What?"

"Centuries ago, Acheron came to me and told me that he'd noticed someone was tampering with the time sequence. He had memories of events that differed from others."

Ambrose cursed. "He knew what I was doing?"

Madoc wavered his hand in a so-so gesture. "He didn't know it was you. All he knew was that things were diverging. But you have to be careful when playing with time."

"It's why the zeitjägers were created," Kody said, interrupting them.

"Exactly. Too many changes and the world becomes unrecognizable." Madoc moved to stand in front of

Nick. "It's not the past you really want to alter. With the exception of your mother, you have no complaints about your past."

Ambrose cleared his throat. "Not entirely true. For the record, there are a lot of stupid things I'd like to undo."

Snorting, Madoc glanced at Kody. "Trust me, Ambrose. Once you and Kody cross paths, you have no complaints about your past." He returned his cold stare to Nick. "What you want to do is stop the deaths of those you love. That's in your futures."

Nick rubbed at the dull ache that was starting to pound in his temple. "I still don't get it." His mom was in his past. Or Ambrose's past.

Kody sucked her breath in. "I think I do. You were all defeated. My father, Acheron, and you. Me. Everyone. Cyprian had won and the world was doomed."

Madoc nodded. "Only one person can defeat a Malachai."

Another Malachai.

"Yeah, but not me," Nick said. "The father loses power around his son, and his presence weakens me, which is how he kicked my butt to begin with." A sad indictment against the curse that was guaranteed to continue to punish the Malachai bloodline.

"Only if you don't have help."

Kody nodded. "That was why Cyprian went after the people he did in our time together, Nick. He was systematically wiping out your allies."

"Neutralizing your allies and family," Madoc corrected her. "The ones who fed Nick's strength and gave him the will to fight."

Nick gaped as he finally understood. "The battle isn't over."

Madoc winked at him. "Exactly. It's just beginning, and because Cyprian went to the past, we know that he needs more power for whatever he's planning. He wants you stronger..."

"To inherit even greater powers." Nick grimaced at the thought.

"That's right. If Cyprian can teach you hate and agony long before you finally succumb to it, the greater his abilities."

Kody scowled. "But he'd already defeated Nick. Cyprian stood alone. He'd won the last battle, and we had lost everything."

Including their lives.

"No, Nyria." Madoc splayed his hand against the wall, and the monitors there flickered. "Your memory's still splotchy."

He showed them an image of their daughter who was speaking to a group of friends Nick remembered from when he'd last gone to the future.

Simi's children, and Kyrian's, stood with their daughter.

But there was one young man he didn't recognize. "Who's the boy next to Simi's daughter?"

"Your son." Madoc's tone was flat and emotionless.

Yet Nick didn't get it. What he said made no sense at all. "That's not Cyprian."

"No. He's your son with Nyria."

Nick gaped as he met Kody's shocked stare. There was something she'd never mentioned to him. "We had a son?"

Eyes wide, she shrugged with an expression every bit as baffled as his probably was.

Madoc nodded. "You're not fighting to save Cyprian. You're fighting to save Bash."

Ambrose sputtered. "How? Why? What? A Malachai has to be born in violence. Those are the rules. We can't have sons unless they're born to replace us."

That was the curse.

Madoc inclined his head to Ambrose. "Nick— or you, rather, Ambrose— broke the curse. I can't tell you how for obvious reasons, but you did. That's how you and Nyria were able to have children without violence and raise them."

Madoc glanced back at the happy faces of the children he'd once known. He still remembered the day he'd first met his half-brother.

Back then, he'd been ambivalent. As a Dream-Hunter, he had siblings in the thousands. One more had never mattered to him.

Not even the Malachai powers had meant anything.

So the two of them had gone their own way for decades.

Until Ambrose had saved the life of Madoc's wife. 'Course, she hadn't been his wife then. But Ambrose had stepped in, with Acheron and Styxx, and protected her when Madoc had been unable to do so.

He never forgot that, and they'd been friends ever since. He owed a debt to Ambrose that he could *never* repay.

It was why he'd been so thrilled when his brother broke his Malachai curse.

Even more thrilled when he'd held Nick's children in his arms. They'd been so incredibly precious. And he'd sworn then to do anything he could to protect them. To protect Ambrose and Nyria.

Then hell had come for them all.

And torn all their lives apart.

Madoc flinched as he saw the future pain that would engulf everyone he loved, and bring them to their knees. "I sometimes wonder if breaking the curse was worth it."

Nick's heart pounded at those grim words. And with that thought, sudden realization struck him like a blow. "That's why Cyprian was born... We broke the curse, and they came after us for it. All because Grim and Laguerre don't like losing."

Madoc slapped him on the back so hard, he stumbled forward. "Give the boy a beignet. He got it. That's exactly what happened. They were livid that you'd cut them out as your generals, and then figured out a way to cut them out of their revenge on your predecessors and progeny."

Nick's head spun with all this new knowledge. He'd broken the curse...

That alone was enough to rattle his senses. The rest...

Incredible.

But it all made sense. Laguerre would have been furious. Her intent had been for the Malachais to pay for abusing her daughter centuries ago. As a goddess of War, her fury never died. Same for her husband. Even for a death god, Grim was a nasty bugger. He'd never take defeat lying down. Or standing up.

For Nick to break that curse, they would have been all over him. Hellbent on revenge.

He met Madoc's gaze. "I would ask when and how I break the curse, but you're not going to tell me, are you?"

"Of course not. If I tell you, you'd probably screw it up."

Nick let out a long sigh at something that would hurt his feelings, if it wasn't true. "So how do we untie this Gordian Knot?"

"You need what you've always relied on."

There was only one thing that could be. It was the one thing he always returned to. Good. Bad. Irritating. They were forever bonded. "My family."

Madoc inclined his head to him. "Exactly. Cyprian's plan is to alienate you. The more pain you feel, the more powers he has."

Great. He was the Energizer Bunny for a son he'd rather not have.

At least you have some use.

God knew that Caleb and the rest had always called him useless, and most of the time, he agreed.

"How do we defeat him?" Kody asked. "Because he creamed us the last time we tried."

Madoc gave her a wry grin. "That's because he picked you off, one at a time."

"Though one may be overpowered, two can defend themselves. A cord of three is not easily broken." Nick could hear his mother saying those words.

"Ecclesiastes 4:12." Ambrose sighed. "Mom and her Bible quotes."

"Yeah. She has one for every occasion." Her faith was unbreakable and unshakable. Sometimes, he envied her that. His faith in everything was hard-won and often doubted.

Without doubt, there can be no real faith. Acheron's favorite saying.

All that solidified Nick's determination. "We have to save them." And the world. "But where do we start?"

Madoc's gaze darkened. "It all ends June 6, 3266."

Kody's eyes filled with pain. "When I was sent back."

Nick remembered his dream where he'd seen himself as a monster Malachai who killed Caleb. When he'd seen Kody die. "My memories merged with Cyprian's." That was the only way to explain what he'd seen.

What he'd felt.

Madoc nodded. "You have the ability to know what he knows, just as he knows you. Cyprian used those memories to destroy the ones closest to you."

Like Stryker would one day try to do. The leader of the Daimon army had used Nick's hatred of Acheron to manipulate him so that Stryker could use Nick to spy on his enemies and find their weaknesses.

For years, that connection had caused Nick to be isolated from his friends and family out of fear of Stryker causing them harm.

But nothing lasted forever.

Not even hatred.

Nick winked at Ambrose. "Guess we part company here, old man."

Ambrose smirked. "No. I'll see you in the future."

"Yeah, it's still screwing with my head." Nick turned toward Madoc. "Can we use one of your portals to get us where we need to go?"

"You can. But be careful. You might have a lot of allies, but you have many more who want you dead."

Some days, that felt like everyone on the planet.

Today, everyone in the universe.

He took Kody's hand, grateful to have her at his side. She'd been so crucial to his sanity for so long now, he couldn't remember a time when she hadn't been there.

"I can't lose you, Kode."

"You're not going to lose me." She smiled up at him before she pulled him in for the best hug he'd ever had. As good as his mom's had been, they were nothing like this. She sank her hand in his hair, and he felt his entire body tremble. How could she both weaken and strengthen him at the same time?

Made no sense, but he couldn't deny what he felt whenever she neared him.

She could bring him to his knees and simultaneously make him fly.

He kissed her lightly before he stepped back and turned to face Madoc. "Send us to the future. Two days after the last battle."

Kody scowled. "Why then?"

"We must have done something after the battle that caused Cyprian to fear us. So much so that he came back to get more power. Means something we do will put fear in him, right?"

"Seems remarkably logical, especially for you." Ambrose turned toward Madoc. "I guess I'll head back to my time."

"What about Caleb and your crew?" Kody asked.

Nick hesitated as he considered that.

Kody frowned at Madoc. "They were all dead when Cyprian killed you."

Which meant they'd be safe to go with him.

Maybe.

"I swear I think my migraine just had a baby."

"Good, it can play with mine." Kody smiled at him.

Madoc shook his head. "I can return you all to

Ambrose's house. Then I'll help the lot of you get where you need to go."

"What about the Fates?" Kody asked. "Won't they have something to say about this?"

Madoc snarled viciously. "I hate those three bitches. If anyone ever wanted them to go down, it's me."

Ambrose scoffed at Madoc. "No. I think it's Acheron or Styxx who'd have the biggest grudge and gripes against them."

"I won't argue that." Madoc waved his hand, and the next thing Nick knew, everything went dark. It felt as if someone grabbed him from behind and jerked him off his feet.

"Ugh, I hate this!" Nick tried to find something to hold on to, but it was useless. *Don't fight it.* It'd only make him more nauseated later. Honestly though, why did it have to be so aggravating?

Portals, time travel, all of it was an awful way to move from one place to another. A chaos demon must have invented it.

But after what seemed like an eternity, he finally stopped falling and found himself back at Ambrose's. He technically landed on his feet. But sadly, the force of it sent him to his knees.

Kody, however, landed like a champ. He'd give her credit. Although she staggered from it, she still managed to stay on her feet. That stagger, though, made him feel a teensy bit better.

Ambrose, of course, had no problems at all. He didn't even flinch as he stuck the landing and then started walking toward his den with that feral lope that let everyone know this was someone who could kick major ass.

"At least I know one day, I'll master this."

Kody smiled. "Baby, you've already mastered it. I think you look hot." She kissed his cheek, then followed after Ambrose.

In that moment, Nick saw a glimmer of a memory. Years from now, Kody was older, but still as stunning.

She'd taken his hand and pulled him after her as they strolled along the Moon Walk in New Orleans.

"You know, Nyria, *your uncle and father are going to kill me."*

Laughing, Kody had given him the same smile. *"Baby, they won't break my heart. Besides, I'm meaner than both of them put together. They taught me all their best tricks."*

Those words had weirdly put the same warm feeling inside him that he felt now. God, how he loved her.

But why did he have that memory?

You need to stop playing with the Eye.

That was probably it. That thing was beyond dangerous.

So's living.

True. Living had been kicking his butt since the day he was born, and there was no letup in sight.

"Hey, boyo!" Aeron stood up as Nick entered Ambrose's den.

"He's back," Caleb added, "but that face... doesn't bode well for any of us."

Nick rolled his eyes at Caleb. "That's because I've signed all of you up to be my sacrificial demons. Hope you're okay with that."

Vawn went even paler. "He's joking, right?"

A tic started in Caleb's cheek. "He's joking, or I'll choke him with his own entrails."

Nick tsked. "Such violence. You need to take a course in anger management, bro."

"I have no problem with anger management. Something makes me angry and I kill it. Problem solved. Trust me, one day you'll make me look lenient." Caleb slid his gaze toward Ambrose, who gave the demon a look that said he was sizing up Caleb's head for his trophy case.

Lovely. He couldn't wait to be that psycho.

"So, what's behind the expression?" Xev asked Nick.

Nick quickly filled them in on everything they'd learned, and on his plan to head to the future.

Xev was aghast as he gestured around the room. "So all of us are dead?"

"No. Neutralized." Kody patted Xev on the back to soothe him. "Cyprian wasn't strong enough to kill anyone other than Nick... and me. The rest of you are in stasis. Our plan is to set you free and fight by your side."

Nick glanced around at his *family*. Though most of them might not be blood related, they were bound just as tightly. And he would die for any of them.

United we stand.

And they were his mighty cord. He knew that. No one would ever break them apart.

Even so, this wasn't going to be easy, but he would see it through. He had no other choice.

"How exactly are you planning to do this?" Caleb asked.

"We go in together as a team and free Acheron first." Kody spoke with a confidence Nick wished he felt.

Caleb arched a brow. "Why Ash?"

That was a simple answer. Nick clicked his teeth and winked at them. "He's the final fate." The harbinger who was supposed to end the world for his goddess mother. So long as Acheron lived, his mother was trapped. It was another reason why Cyprian hadn't dared to kill him. That would have unleashed the power that had birthed their Malachai line thousands upon thousands of years ago.

Apollymi didn't play when it came to the death of her son. To this day, she hated the gods for what they'd done to Nick's progenitor.

And after everything humanity and the gods had done to Acheron...

If she were ever freed, the whole world would burn. As powerful as a Malachai was, they still couldn't compete with the original goddess who'd birthed their line.

She was the one thing everyone with a brain feared.

And while the first Malachai may have been her son, that was so long ago that she would see them dead if they harmed one hair on Acheron's head.

Acheron was her direct son. They were just her great times a thousand grandsons.

"Where do we—"

Xev's question was cut off as the door opened to reveal a tall, scary beast of a man— or demon would probably be a closer description.

Takeshi.

Acheron had once told him that Takeshi hadn't invented war. He'd perfected it.

Tall and sleek, Takeshi was known as the *Ichikagi. First*

Shadow. How he'd become a zeitjäger, Nick still didn't know. But they were the keepers of time. It was their job to make sure no one abused a timeline or altered one.

They also stole time away from others and used it to barter. Zeitjägers were very scary beasts.

Even so, Nick wasn't afraid of his old friend.

"T." Nick inclined his head. "What's up?"

"Ambrose tells me that you're planning to do something profoundly stupid."

"He's breathing, isn't he?" Caleb asked. "That means he's naturally planning something stupid. Sadly, we can't seem to curb that tendency."

Takeshi smirked at Caleb. "Given your history, I'm sure you've tried."

Caleb held his hands up in surrender. "Hey, just be glad I'm not your favorite kitsune, right?"

"Do not go there, demon. I'm not in the mood."

Nick frowned at their exchange. "What kitsune?"

"Doesn't matter." Takeshi's tone told him that any further questioning might result in a maiming.

"It matters," Caleb whispered. "Think of it like the Caleb to the Malachai."

Ah, that explained it. Takeshi had his own irritant who was missing. Good to know.

Or maybe not. It kind of scared Nick to know that

there were more irritating beasts in the world than just the ones he knew.

Takeshi put his hands on his hips as he surveyed their group with an expression that said he was less than pleased. "So you want me to take the Scooby crew to the future?"

Nick grinned at him. "You already did that, *cher*."

"And the weight of you all doing that practically broke my back. What in this unholy universe makes you think for one minute that I'll do it again?"

"Because I'm cute and cuddly."

Groaning, Takeshi rolled his eyes. "Kody? You could do so much better for a boyfriend."

"That's what everyone, including Nick, keeps telling me. But Nick's right. He's kudzu. The longer you hang around him, the more he grows on you."

Takeshi passed a pained grimace toward Nick. "Please don't grow on me."

"I'll try not to, but I am irresistibly delicious."

Laughing, Takeshi shook his head. "I pity your friends and family... Anyway, I should probably take you home."

Nick tsked. "Been there. Done that. I'm thinking we need to go further into the future."

"I think you're going to get me killed." Takeshi let out

a long, exasperated sigh. "And Madoc will owe me a tremendous favor for doing this for you. Lazy beast."

In that moment, Nick saw an image in his mind of the ancient being in his samurai armor. No wonder people, gods, and demons had trembled before him.

All except his son.

His son had never taken him seriously. It was why Nick got away with what he did. In Takeshi's mind, he reminded him of the boy he'd lost long ago.

Nick batted his lashes. "Please, Mr. Badbutt. I promise I'll be good. I'll eat my veggies and go to bed when you tell me to."

Takeshi narrowed his eyes. "Don't make me slap you."

"Won't work," Caleb said. "Trust me. It only makes him worse."

Takeshi arched a brow. "Personal experience?"

"Oh yeah."

Takeshi laughed again. "Where is it you think you need to be?"

Kody stepped forward. "3266."

Takeshi's eyes widened as he digested her request. "BC?"

"AD."

Several emotions went over Takeshi's face. Confusion. Anger. Bewilderment.

He settled on disgust. "Why?"

"To stop the Cyprian Malachai," Kody answered simply.

That only seemed to baffle Takeshi more. "What makes you think that'll work?"

Nick grinned. "It hasn't not worked yet."

Takeshi pressed his hand to his forehead at Nick's comment. It was a reaction that a lot of people had to him. As if he were giving them a brain tumor. "Keep that optimism, kid. It might not help you in the future."

"What?"

"Exactly."

Nick laughed as he realized Takeshi had caught on and played him right back. It was awesome.

"So, are you willing to take us there?" he asked.

Takeshi paused before he answered. "I still don't know how I let Madoc talk me into this. And I want it on record that I am a conscientious objector."

Caleb snorted. "I want it on record that I'm a conscientious objector to all of Nick's idiocy."

"I'm inclined to agree. Yet here we are... unwilling participants." Takeshi sighed. "So who all the victims going with me?"

"Everyone except Ambrose."

Shock spread across Takeshi's face, then he visibly

shivered. "Really? He's the voice of reason? You really are doomed."

Xev snorted. "Like we didn't know that already?" He took a step toward Kody. "What do we have to look forward to in that time period, Miss Kody?"

"Faster internet."

Nick liked the sound of that. "Awesome! I need more bandwidth. When can we leave?"

Takeshi leaned forward and whispered darkly into Nick's ear, "Be careful what you wish for... you just might get it."

5

NEW ORLEANS, 3266

Kody froze as they appeared where Nick's home had once stood. It was one thing to remember this, but another to be back here.

In the flesh.

Unreasoning horror went through her as she relived the nightmare of her past. As she saw the awful fighting that had taken place all around this corner. Buildings had been on fire. People had been running and screaming, calling out for someone to help them.

There had been no help for anyone.

With a sickening glee that continued to haunt her, Cyprian had picked them off, one by one.

Ambrose had shielded her from the demons that were out to kill anyone in their path. "Get to safety."

He'd made it sound so easy. Yet she couldn't leave him to deal with this chaos and madness. "What about you?"

"I will *never* leave you. I'm always with you."

Until he wasn't.

She could still feel the pain of his death. Feel the pain of her own. That final breath when she'd known all was lost. That there would be no future for them. That all their dreams and everything they'd built together and planned for was for nothing.

Evil had conquered them and destroyed everything they'd done their best to protect.

And there had been nothing she could do to stop it.

Kody winced as tears filled her eyes from the pain of everything. Why couldn't she purge these nightmares? It was so hard to move on when the pain was still fresh. Still paralyzing.

How could her entire life have been negated and destroyed by one sick psycho?

It wasn't right or fair. And she'd never understand why the Malachai had been cursed. Why Cyprian couldn't have been like Nick. Forgiving.

Decent.

Human.

She wiped at her tears before others saw them. It

really sucked to know their futures and not be able to warn them.

Or stop it.

"Where's my house?" Nick staggered toward the remains. All that was left was the burned-out debris. Pieces of lumber, twisted wrought iron, and charred memories of a horrible battle.

Kody swallowed the lump of grief in her throat. "Cyprian and his army. They attacked and torched it because they knew it'd devastate you."

"He was right." Nick raked his hands through his hair. "I am devastated. What a bahs— monster"

Wanting to ease the pain in his eyes, Kody moved to hug him, but he wouldn't let her.

Nick was too busy trying to absorb this. To cope with a reality that had brought her to her knees.

After a few seconds, he held his hands up. "All right. I'm shrugging this off. There's nothing we can do about it. And right now, we have much more important things to focus on."

"Find Acheron." Xev toed at the dust. "Hope he wasn't in the house."

Nick grimaced at Xev's light tone. "You're not funny."

"Really? Everyone else laughed... Even Kody."

"I'm not laughing." But really, she had. Clearing her

throat to disguise her amusement, Kody started toward the street.

"You know where he is?" Nick asked.

"Not exactly."

Caleb followed her. "What do you mean, *not exactly*? Don't tell me we just followed you through time for a *not exactly*."

Kody turned around to face them. "I know where he was taken."

"And that would be?" Caleb asked.

"Cyprian's lair."

All of the men stopped moving.

"Wait... what?" Nick gaped at her.

She offered him a smile. "You didn't think this would be easy, did you?"

Nick rubbed at the back of his neck. "Yeah. Little bit. I figured we're owed some."

"Doom... despair... rain agony on me."

Nick grimaced as Caleb broke into that old song his mom used to sing all the time. "Don't want to hear it, Cay."

"Don't want to live it, Nick. And yet—" He gestured at the destruction around them. "Here we are."

Vawn raised his hands. "Those of us who are about to die... do *not* salute you."

Kaziel barked.

"Exactly," Caleb said to Kaziel.

"What?" Nick asked.

Vawn smirked. "He says he'd salute, but right now he's missing his hand and the middle finger he'd like to salute you with."

"Behave, Lassie, or I'll feed you some stale Alpo." Nick turned around in a slow circle to get his bearings. Nothing was familiar. The entire city looked like a war zone. "What happened here?"

"Ambrose told you. Everything just kept getting worse. By the time I was born, humans had become savage. Lack of regard for everyone and everything took its toll. They tore down the cities, then moved outward until there was nothing left. No resources. No protection. No laws. Nothing. It was like something out of a bad sci-fi movie." Kody sighed as she looked over the devastation. "Those with the means went into seclusion and left the rest to battle it out."

"But not the Dark-Hunters." Nick remembered that much from the Eye.

"No. They stayed so that they could ride herd on the demons who just kept cropping up to add to the madness. They're still fighting to save what little bit of humanity exists."

Caleb scowled. "What about the Daimons?" They

were the soul-stealing demons the Dark-Hunters had originally been created to police.

She slid her gaze to Nick, then finally answered. "After the Daimons regained their ability to walk in daylight and formed an alliance with the Dark-Hunters—"

"They what?" Nick was stunned by that.

Kody held her hand up and chuckled over the amazing turnaround that her brother, Urian, had spent years telling her about. Due to some interesting history, Urian had started out in life as a Daimon only to be saved by her uncle, Acheron, who'd had no idea at the time that they were related. "Long story, but they became allies and fought with us." She toed at a piece of broken masonry. "They're still here. Or at least some of them are."

Nick struggled to digest that. "Enemies become friends and friends become enemies."

"Nature of the beast." Caleb looked poignantly at Xev, who nodded in agreement. "It's why I don't make friends."

Xev cracked a wry grin. "You never know what will change your heart toward someone. All it took for me was one sight of Myone. She altered my point of view on most everything, and forever changed my world."

Caleb nodded. "It took a bit longer for me, but

Lilliana did the same. I saw the world through her eyes, and I liked her perspective a lot more than mine. All I wanted was to be the human she thought I was."

Which said a lot, given he was a demon through and through.

"And here we are." Nick stared out at the waste and destruction all around them.

"Picking up the pieces of the past, and trying to make a better future." Kody moved to stand next to him.

Nick wanted to hate her ever optimistic view, but sadly, it was what he normally loved most about her.

Not wanting to hurt her feelings, he changed the subject. "How far is Cyprian's lair?"

Before Kody could respond, a loud screech sounded.

Ducking his head out of habit, Nick widened his eyes. "Hell monkeys?"

A burst of fire came out of nowhere, so close it singed part of the hair on Nick's arm.

Caleb tossed up a shield to protect them as the flames danced outside his invisible wall. While it was pretty, the heat was almost as excruciating as being burned alive.

Almost.

This was why Nick didn't want to go to hell. Heat like this was utter misery. Like New Orleans in August... only hotter and more biting.

Nick wiped at the sweat on his brow. "Not to be a downer, but anyone have an idea on how to get out of this one?"

Vawn's eyes turned a vibrant orange that reminded Nick of Caleb's when he was in demon form. "Hold your ears."

Before Nick could ask what Vawn had planned, Vawn shifted into a whiff of smoke to drift out of the bubble.

Then it came, that soul-shattering banshee scream.

The fire diminished. Nick's eardrums were on the verge of bursting when the fire stopped, and blood splashed over the shield.

Vawn approached them with a wide grin. "Path cleared. Demon exploded. Hope your ears aren't ringing too much, me lovelies."

Nick's were howling, but he knew from experience they would stop eventually.

Or his head would explode much the same way the demon's had. At the moment, he wasn't sure if that wouldn't be better than the pain shooting through his skull.

Shaking his head, he smirked at Vawn. "You enjoy your evil way too much."

"And you don't enjoy yours nearly enough. Embrace

the inner demon, lad. Makes life much more interesting."

So said Vawn. But Nick totally disagreed. "Yeah, no. That just seems like a frightening way to live."

"As I said, it makes life much more interesting."

Nick snorted. "My life gets any more interesting, it'll probably kill me."

Caleb sucked his breath through his teeth. "Kid has a point. I'd like to try a little boredom for a minute or a few months... years preferably."

"Back on track?" Kody motioned over her shoulder. "We need to get to someone's lair. Remember?"

"Sorry." Nick rubbed at his ears. "Demon entrails always distract me. Where are we going, exactly?"

Kody didn't say a word as she led them several blocks over.

Nick winced as they passed his old school where they'd all spent some good and bad times. Even though he'd just been there in his own time period, it seemed as long ago as the thousands of years that separated his human life from this one.

Like his home where they'd just been, there was nothing left. Not even a single brick or piece of the old parking lot. All that remained of his high school was a crater.

Well take that back, there was one old post left from

where the fence used to be. A single, solitary post perched about a foot away from the crater.

For some reason, it seemed as if that should be poignant or meaningful. Maybe he was just looking for some rhyme or reason to this anarchy and destruction.

Not wanting to think about it, he followed her a little farther. To a shop that looked oddly familiar.

No. *Really* familiar.

It couldn't be...

Kody opened the door and then held it for him to enter. Stunned, Nick stepped inside and took in the zombie posters and bows, along with ads for cyber-implants.

All that would be shocking enough. But the grumbling voice of Bubba Burdette as he came out of the back of the shop to greet them riveted Nick's feet to the floor.

Was this for real?

"Bubba?"

"Nick?"

They spoke simultaneously.

His mind whirling, Nick staggered forward to hug the huge beast of a man. Like his Dark-Hunter boss Kyrian, Bubba had been a father figure to him. Always there. Always caring, teaching him life lessons and helping him watch over his mom. Okay, Bubba hasn't been selfless in that action as he was dating Nick's mom, but still...

Bubba had always been kicking his tail whenever Nick needed it.

Though they stood even in height, Bubba had the kind of muscular build Nick would kill for. With black hair and blue eyes, Bubba Burdette was the man Nick had wanted to be. Caring. Kind. Funny.

Kickass.

Granted, Bubba had a crazy streak that was bigger than the Pontchartrain. But the zombie-hunting thing aside, he was classic.

Nick just couldn't believe he was here, in front of him. "You're still alive? How?"

Stepping back, Bubba grinned. "Hard to kill." He swept his gaze over Nick's body. "How are you here? As a kid?"

"Time travel. How are you still alive? Aren't you, like, nine million years old?"

Bubba rolled his eyes. "Not Fred Flintstone, buddy." He screwed his face up. "Then again, I am over a thousand years old at this point. Maybe I am Cro-mag."

"Troglodyte." Nick had to use Bubba's favorite insult for people.

He laughed at the reference. "I've missed you, Nick."

He cupped him on the back of the neck and drew him in to kiss the top of his head.

"Is Mark here, too?"

Mark Fingerman had been Bubba's best friend and sidekick. Together, they'd gotten into all kinds of crap. Amusing, insane crap that had always made Nick laugh.

Sadness clouded those deep blue eyes. "Mark died long ago. He was human."

"And you?"

Bubba held his arms out. The moment he did, a huge span of wings came out of his back. "Necrodemian."

Nick gaped at the revelation. Necrodemians chased after certain classes of demons and returned them to their respective planes of existence. They were also part of the same group that had brought Kody back from the dead and sent her after him.

He would be more shocked, except for one thing...

"You took your father's place?"

Bubba winced as his wings vanished. "After he was killed in a battle. Yeah."

Dang. That made Nick's stomach ache. He'd loved Dr. Bruce. Like Bubba, he'd been a good man with a good heart. And Nick had found out the hard way that Dr. Bruce was a Necrodemian. The old man had actually gone after him, until Nick had proven that he wasn't an evil Malachai.

He chose peace over war.

Even so, it'd taken Dr. Bruce a minute to warm up to him and realize Nick had no intention of ending the world.

Or anyone else.

"I'm sorry, Bubba."

"It's okay. You tried to save him, and that I'll never forget." A smile returned to Bubba's face as he saw the others. "Been a while, Caleb. Xev."

One by one, he shook everyone's hands.

Until he got to Kody. "What happened to you, Nyria? You look like you're aging backwards."

It took Nick a second to realize that Bubba had known Kody twice in his life. As "Kody," Nick's high school sweetheart and then as Nyria in her real body during the time period when she'd been Nick's wife.

Yeah, this was screwing with his head again. "Nyria *is* Kody."

Bubba scowled. "No. Kody looked different. It might have been a few hundred years, but I remember her clearly."

"I'm Kody *and* Nyria."

His scowl deepened. "I don't understand. You both died."

Lifting her hands, she turned a small circle and smiled. "Like a Dark-Hunter. Can't keep a good woman down."

"Apparently not, and I'm grateful for that fact." He pulled her in for a hug. "It's so good to see you." He cracked a grin at her. "Both of you."

"You, too." She stepped back to smile up at him. "I've missed all of you so much."

"Yeah." Bubba rubbed her arm, then looked toward Nick. "So, why are all of you here?"

"I'd say bad luck, but..." Nick turned back to Kody. "You want to explain?"

"We're looking for Cyprian's lair."

Well, straight to the point. He'd expected a little more finesse. He should have known better. Kody always told it like it was.

Feelings be darned. She always ripped the band-aid straight off the skin.

Bubba stiffened. "Why?"

Nick shrugged with feigned nonchalance. "We're profoundly stupid. Why else?"

Laughing, Bubba nodded. "To go *there*, I'd have to agree. What *are* you thinking?"

"We help Acheron escape. Maybe fight a demon or two and don't die." Nick grinned.

"That the plan?" Bubba asked.

Aeron cleared his throat. "Aye. Especially the *don't die* part. I'm rather all about it."

Xev nodded. "I also vote that we add a no-torture clause. Been there, done that, and I really don't recommend a repeat... It's not shampoo. And I have enough t-shirts."

Snorting, Nick turned the subject back to the important part. "Anyway, I'm thinking this is a chess game, and we need to rescue our king."

"Wait... I'm not sure about that analogy. If Acheron is king, wouldn't that make my father the queen?"

Nick grinned at Kody. "Co-kings?"

"On my father's behalf, thank you."

"You're most welcome."

Aeron cleared his throat. "For the record, it should be noted that the queen is the most powerful piece on a chessboard. It goes wherever it wants, with no restrictions."

Kody frowned at that. "Interesting. Maybe my dad is the queen then."

Xev snorted. "That's sounds more like Acheron, if you ask me."

"Does it really matter?" Bubba asked.

They turned to face him.

His expression grim, Bubba let out a long, tired

breath. "Look, I'm having PTSD. I'll take you there, but if Cyprian catches us..."

"He won't," Nick said with a confidence he didn't really feel.

"What makes you so sure?"

"He thinks we're in the past. I'm hoping by the time he realizes we've gone forward, we'll have Acheron back."

"And if he figures it out sooner?"

"That's why I'm Catholic, Bubba." Nick crossed himself. "I have faith and prayer."

Sadness darkened Bubba's eyes. "You sound so much like your mama."

Nick sobered as he realized what he'd inadvertently done. Bubba had dated his mom for years. The two of them had loved each other. Deeply. But Bubba's fear of making his mom a target had kept him from marrying her.

Likewise, his mother's fear of happiness had kept her from wanting to marry. Every time anything good happened in her life, she'd had an equal or worse dose of bad.

I always pay for my happiness, Nicky. Sometimes, the price is just too high, and I've had enough of it. I just can't risk any more hurt.

Funny how people manifested their fears. His mom

and Bubba had been so afraid of losing each other that they had stayed apart.

Had Bubba been there that night...

His mom would still be alive.

Even so, Nick didn't blame Bubba. Her death was on his head, alone. Even though he had blamed Acheron for it for years, he knew the truth.

He'd been the one who'd left her on a night when he should have stayed by her side. He'd known the dangers. Known what wanted to kill him.

And he'd left her to fend for herself against a demon.

After all she'd sacrificed to keep and raise him, he'd failed her.

Don't think about it.

But it was hard. You never, ever got over things. You just got through them. The sting of it was always there to burn you to the core. All time did was allow you to come to terms with the bad and design a better way to cope.

Past mistakes were haunting, no matter how many years passed. No matter how much he wanted to forget. He kept playing out scenarios.

Would have. Should have. Could have.

They were the real enemies of life. The true demons

that haunted everyone. If only there was some exorcism for them.

We all make mistakes. They're easy. It's learning to live with them that's hard. Life will test you and bring you to your knees, over and over again. That's when you have to go deep, catch your breath, and raise one finger and one fist to the Fates. Come get some, bitches. 'Cause I'm not going down. Not today. Not tomorrow. Not ever. You stand up, Nick, and you fight with everything you have. That's when you know you're a real warrior. Anyone can fight when they're winning. It's finding the courage to stand after life has beaten you down that makes you a hero.

To this day, he could hear Acheron's words. They'd been powerful and had helped him through so many crises.

Never give up. Never surrender.

Acheron was forever quoting *Galaxy Quest*. *I should never have seen that with him.* But that night had been one of Nick's favorite memories. It was the first time he'd actually heard Acheron laugh like a kid. He'd been so used to Acheron the Serious... But that night, Acheron had acted like the twenty-one-year-old he appeared to be.

So many good memories. He glanced to Kody, and warmth spread through him. That was the thing. How she made him feel. No matter how bad his day was, all he had to do was feel her near him, touch or see her face and everything was made better.

Bubba chucked him on the shoulder, bringing his thoughts back to the matter at hand. "You remember my zombie lessons, kid?"

"Yeah, why?"

"None of them will help with this journey."

"Oh, awesome. Then why are you bringing it up?"

"I like screwing with people. What we're fighting, you'll have to decapitate to kill. Or worse."

Nick screwed his face up. "Ew!"

"Yeah." Bubba went to the back of his store and returned with his sword. "Everyone armed?"

Nick pulled his Malachai sword hilt from his pocket, then expanded it. "Yep."

Bubba looked at Aeron and Vawn. With a flick of the hand, Vawn exposed five razor-sharp claws. "I don't need a sword."

Aeron grinned. "I prefer to use me fangs. I like tasting the blood of me enemies. I find it keeps me young."

Nick winced at the image in his mind. Unlike Bubba, he knew they weren't joking. That little Trinity of Death liked getting down and dirty. He was so glad they were on his side.

When Bubba looked at Xev, Xev elbowed Caleb. "We

both like ripping the heads off things, especially when they come at us."

"Yeah," Caleb agreed. "I don't need no stinking sword."

"Very well." Bubba spread his hand out and manifested a portal in his store.

Nick groaned. "Ugh!" He looked up at the ceiling. "Why Lord, why another portal? I hate these things!"

"That's why you're going first." Caleb tossed him in.

By the time Nick started protesting, he was already through it. Which wasn't really fair. He'd wanted to complain.

Like Aeron had said, it kept him young.

But as he looked around, all those thoughts skidded to a halt. This was not what he'd expected from a Malachai lair. Instead of being grim and dark, it was remarkably...

Perky.

It looked more like something Simi would have picked out as her home. Bright sun. Woodsy.

Weird. Definitely weird.

Nick turned around as Kody, Caleb, Vawn, Xev, Kaziel, Aeron, and Bubba joined him. They looked as confused by their surroundings as he felt.

"Are we in the right place?" Caleb asked.

Bubba smirked. "Yes."

His eyes widened. "This is certainly a step up." He hit Nick in the stomach. "Why couldn't you ever pick a place like this?"

"Because the country scares me."

Caleb's eyebrow lifted. "You live in New Orleans, one of the most crime-ridden cities in America. How in the name of Artemis could you *ever* be afraid of country living?"

Offended, Nick stiffened. "Hey now, I know what criminals will do and how it feels to be shot. Animals..."

"Can't shoot you from a hundred yards away?" Xev asked.

Nick gave him a dry stare. "They're unpredictable and they can rip my throat out. Speaking from personal experience, I'd rather be shot."

Vawn snorted. "Says the man who travels with two wolves." Vawn petted Kaziel. "Trust me, they're a lot easier to deal with than people, demons, or gods. They don't betray you, and they only bite when provoked. I've never known one to smile at your face, then go for your back."

That was a sad indictment against humanity. True, but sad nonetheless.

Bubba unsheathed his sword. "Word to the wise—nothing here is what it seems. Heads up and watch your step. Pretty much everything we pass will try to kill you."

"So it's just another day." Nick smiled at him.

Shaking his head, Bubba started forward with a caution in his steps that let Nick know he wasn't kidding or exaggerating. When Bubba went into zombie mode, it was always serious.

And scary.

"Where are we?" Nick asked.

"Azmodea."

His jaw went slack at that. "No. No way." Azmodea was a dank, awful place. Like something in a bad horror movie... or Disney's *Haunted Mansion*. "I thought everything here was dark and terrifying."

"Not always." Caleb transformed to his demonic form. "But like this... it means this land was conquered by someone or something. How did they defeat Noir and Azura?"

"They're not defeated."

Xev and Caleb exchanged a confused stare as if they didn't believe Bubba's words.

In spite of his earlier words, Caleb drew his sword. "Neither of them would ever go for this. They like a dark night too much."

"True," Bubba agreed. "Cyprian opened the gates. They took the human world, and Cyprian took this one."

Caleb scoffed. "Cyprian didn't strike me as a happy-go-lucky, *My Little Pony* kind of guy."

Bubba gave him a dry stare. One he raked over Caleb's demonic body. "Looks can be deceiving and Cyprian is a god of deception."

Those words made Nick sick to his stomach. And it explained so much. No wonder the human world looked like it did. Someone had let out the darkest powers of the universe to run roughshod over it.

Mankind would have had no idea how to fight them. Or how to survive.

Why, Lord? Why? He repeated.

Xev's mouth opened and closed as if he was struggling with words.

Finally, he spoke. "What about Thorn?"

Bubba shook his head sadly. "He went down in the battle. Fighting for you guys."

"Thorn is dead?" Kody's eyes welled with tears.

"No. He's captured. Noir would never be able to kill his son. Believe it or not."

But he'd be able to torture him. That was the saddest and sickest part. Noir was an animal.

She moved over to Nick. "We have to set this right."

"I know, *cher.* That's why we're here." Too bad he couldn't see anything more than utter defeat for all of them.

How in the world were they supposed to make this

right?

Aeron quickened his steps. "For the record, I still think it'd be better to stop Cyprian from being born."

"Won't help," Caleb said to him. "The more you try to thwart destiny, the more you screw it up."

Xev agreed. "There's a time to fight and a time to yield."

"I yielded once." Vawn gestured at his female body. "Didn't turn out well for me. It's why I no longer give up ground."

Nick felt so bad for his companion. "Is there any way to reverse your curse?"

"None that I've found."

"We should put that on the list."

Caleb laughed. "Sure, kid. Kill Cyprian. Free Acheron and the others. Save the world and give Vawn back the body that was taken. Anything else you want to add?"

"Yeah. Cure my demon protector of his sarcasm."

Kody tsked. "Now, now. You'd miss it if it was gone."

Nick cut a grimace toward Caleb. "I'm willing to make that sacrifice."

"Shh!" Bubba held up his hand.

Nick froze, unsure what had made Bubba nervous. Then he heard it. The sound of what seemed to be a thousand wings coming toward them.

"What is that?" he whispered.

"Hit the trees!" Bubba ran for the dense forest.

Nick took a second to process that. Then he realized they'd left him behind.

Jerks!

Heading to the trees, he quickly tucked himself back into the group. But what he wanted to do was yell at them for not looking back.

Seriously? Not even Kody had paused to make sure he was with them.

I don't have to outrun the bear, bro. I just have to outrun you. For once, he didn't find that old joke funny.

You know you're the Malachai, right?

True, but there are still things that can hurt me.

The sound grew louder.

Closer.

And for all he knew, those were things that could do all manner of damage to him.

Everyone did their best to blend into the forest.

Except Nick. He knew that there was no way for him to vanish into the foliage.

Awesome. Thanks, Mom, for the fluorescent shirt! It doesn't blend. Ever.

Knowing he was a walking billboard for whatever was heading their way, Nick wanted desperately to repeat his question to Bubba about what was coming here to eat him. But the wild look in Bubba's eyes told him to stay silent.

He ran through his mind every threat he knew and that they'd faced. Hell monkeys. Demons. Gallu... You name it. And still nothing came to mind.

Until he saw them.

The sky was dark with red-skinned demons, crows, and ravens. That wasn't as terrifying as he'd thought. "Wow... it's a thousand Calebs."

Caleb grimaced at him. "I'm not the only Daeva in existence."

Apparently. Some of them had the same orange hair with yellow serpent eyes and fangs that Caleb did. But it was the deep blood-red skin and black wings that always made Nick cringe. Because it reminded him of his own demonic form. How hideous he felt whenever he shifted into his Malachai body. Forget puberty, that form was a lot harder to acclimate to than body hair growing in weird places.

And like a Malachai, the Daeva could shapeshift, which was why a large number of them were in crow or raven form.

"Any of them friends?"

Caleb shook his head. "Daeva don't have friends. Just allies or enemies."

Made sense given what he knew of the beasts. But it

still didn't answer Nick's question. "Any of them your former soldiers?"

"Yeah. But that doesn't make them allies at the moment. I don't know who they follow."

"Why are there so many?" Kody whispered.

Caleb shrugged. "Don't know. We don't usually congregate in a large number unless we're fighting. A murder of Daeve tends to make folks nervous and the gods get twitchy."

"Which means someone's leading them." Xev moved closer to Bubba. "Any ideas on whom that might be?"

"I'd say they're under Cyprian's command. Once he emerged as the Malachai, he subjugated every demon he could find."

Then it made sense they were in his son's army.

"Great." Nick started to stand when he heard them coming right at them.

See, Ma! The shirt is worse than a lighthouse.

Kaziel jumped on top of him, forcing him back to the ground and covering his hideous shirt with his body.

Okay, Vawn was right. The Cŵn Annwn was loyal to a fault.

"Thank you, Scooby." Nick patted him on the head and was grateful for the assist.

At least until Kaziel sneezed on him.

"Uh! Really, dude?" Nick regretted speaking the

moment the disgusted words left his lips.

Because it notified the demonic herd where they were.

Xev cursed. "Sneeze on him again."

"Bite him!" Vawn growled.

En masse, the demons descended from the sky to land in the woods around them.

Great. Just what they needed. It was raining blood-thirsty demons. All they needed next was a light dusting of hell monkeys followed by hailing brimstone.

"Run?" Nick asked.

"Only if you want to be chased down and murdered." Caleb had them form a circle. "Hold fast and don't fight until I say."

Nick had never felt more naked or exposed than he did right now as a huge group of those demons landed in an even larger circle around his group. That was bad enough, but a bunch more who were in their crow and raven forms perched in the trees.

Rising to his feet, he stepped closer to Kody. "I saw this movie once. It didn't end well for the humans. And I'm not Tippi Hedren. No idea how to row a boat or run in heels."

Caleb rolled his eyes, but didn't comment on Nick's reference to *The Birds*. "Who leads you?" he asked the demons.

A female Daeva approached. Nick was completely mesmerized. He'd always thought Caleb looked a bit gross in his demonic form, yet there was something compelling about this one. She had perfectly formed features. Beautiful, really. Her orange hair was pulled back from her face in intricate braids that had to be created with magic. Otherwise, it would take more time than he could imagine to create such an elaborate hairdo.

And the one thing he knew about the demons he'd met— they lacked patience.

White and gold armor covered curves that were quite spectacular and made him feel guilty for even noticing. Good thing Kody couldn't hear or read his thoughts. Otherwise, he'd have been slapped by now. And rightfully so.

She held a sword angled toward Caleb's throat. A snarl curled her lips as she narrowed those yellow eyes on him. "Traitor!"

Caleb dropped his sword and held his hands up. "It's not like that, Lyseah."

That only made her angrier. "You disgust me! How could you?"

"The same way you stood over me when I was punished. You said nothing in my defense."

"I hated you and was glad to see you beaten! I still hate you!"

"Then call for my death and let the others with me live."

She sneered even more as she looked at each of them in turn. "Still siding with the humans, I see."

"What!" That howl of outrage went through all of them at once.

Caleb laughed. "Look closer, love. There's not a human among my friends."

Her sword went from Caleb to Bubba. "Worse. A Necrodemian."

As soon as her sword was pointed elsewhere, Caleb lunged at her and disarmed her.

With a feral shriek of outrage, she punched at his throat. Caleb caught her wrist and twisted her arm behind her back. She stomped his foot, then headbutted him.

They moved in to help.

"Stay out of this!" Caleb wiped the blood from his lips and went to grab her again.

Until she punched him in the face.

Nick winced in sympathy. That had to hurt.

It didn't appear to faze Caleb at all. His nose bleeding, he ducked her next attack, then swept her feet out from under her.

Before she could recover, Caleb pinned her to the ground.

She bucked against him as he managed to hold her fast. "Let me go!"

"Listen to me!"

"Why? So you can lie?"

"I never lied to you."

Tears misted in her eyes. "You said you loved *me*! It was a lie!"

Shame descended over Caleb's face. Visibly wincing, he moved his weight from her. "It wasn't a lie. I meant it."

She shoved him back. "So you loved me, but married a human? A human!" she repeated. "How could you?"

"I don't know. It just happened."

With another earsplitting scream, she flipped him to his back and held a knife to his throat. "I should kill you for your betrayal."

"If it eases your pain, do it."

Nick wanted to protest, but honestly, he felt like a voyeur. This was a personal matter and something Caleb had *never* talked about.

And here he'd thought Lilliana was the only woman in Caleb's life. He'd never once considered that Caleb had been with a demon.

Stupid in retrospect. He should have known Caleb

would have been with someone other than his wife. A lot of someones. Demons and otherwise. That made much more sense, really.

As he watched, he fully expected the demon to cut Caleb's throat.

Instead, she stood and then kicked him in the ribs. "You should have died in the war."

Rubbing where she'd kicked him, Caleb rolled to his feet. "What are you doing here, Seah?"

"None of your business. You're not one of us. You haven't been one of us since you chose the humans over your own kind."

A male stepped forward. "Not true. He serves the Malachai, just like we do."

She raked another sneer over the demon who'd spoken. "You defend him?"

The demon shrugged. "Well, he is my brother."

"*Half*-brother." Lyseah glared at Caleb. "Just because you shared a mother, doesn't make you family."

Nick turned to Kody and mouthed, *Brother?*

Eyes wide, she shrugged.

There was something else he hadn't considered. That either Xev or Caleb would have siblings they hadn't mentioned. But again, that made sense.

Their parents had been known for getting around. Given that, there was no telling how many siblings they had. Probably some they'd never met or knew existed themselves.

The male demon moved closer to Caleb. "I think he's suffered enough without us adding to it. It's good to see you again, Malphas."

Caleb held his hand out to him. "You too, Itzal."

Itzal took his hand, then jerked him into his arms. "I should stab you through the heart."

"Wouldn't be a family reunion without bloodshed."

Snorting, Itzal shoved him back. "Who are these interlopers who travel with you?"

Caleb introduced everyone until he got to Nick. He hesitated.

"He's a Malachai." It wasn't a question. Itzal made the declaration without any judgment.

Caleb nodded.

That only confused them, as they knew Nick shouldn't be here, given that Cyprian was still alive.

"You're Cyprian's son?" Lyseah finally asked.

"His father," Caleb answered before Nick had a chance.

"Impossible."

Nick grinned at her. "Apparently not. Here I stand in my hideous shirt."

Itzal cocked his head as if he was struggling to understand. "So who do we serve now? Malachai I or

Malachai II?" He looked at Lyseah. "Ambrose commanded us before Cyprian. And if this is Ambrose, shouldn't we be following his orders instead of Cyprian's?"

She used her telekinesis to retrieve her sword from the ground. Without hesitating, she moved toward Nick. "This isn't Ambrose."

Waving his hand, Xev used his powers to turn her sword away from Nick's throat. "Not yet. But he will become Ambrose. As such…"

"We're bound to him," Itzal finished.

Nick looked to Caleb. "Does this mean we have an army?"

"Maybe." Caleb turned to Lyseah. "Who's the leader?"

"I am." Her tone defied Caleb. "They promoted me after *your* betrayal."

"I didn't betray you."

"No, Malphas. You betrayed us all."

Caleb raked his hands through his hair in utter frustration. "I fell in love, Seah. I'm sorry if that offends. But I never meant to hurt you."

"Keep telling yourself those lies. You might believe them. But *I* know the truth." She pulled a necklace off and threw it at him.

His expression stone, he caught it in his fist.

Nick started to say that if she'd kept a memento from Caleb, she couldn't really hate him. Otherwise, she'd have thrown it out centuries ago.

Then his common sense did what it seldom did— it rose up and kept his mouth shut.

"Caleb?"

Caleb didn't answer Kody as he struggled with the pain he felt. His love of Lil had blocked out everything else in his life.

Everything except the way Lyseah had stood by as he was dragged and beaten over the fact that he'd sided with humans. Over the fact he'd fallen in love.

She'd stood by as he was personally enslaved to the Malachai who'd taken even less mercy on him.

That callousness had killed any lingering love in his heart for her. But obviously, she had never forgotten.

Or forgiven.

He looked down at the amber necklace he'd given her so very long ago.

For protection whenever he wasn't with her.

"Lyseah?" He went after her as she stormed away.

Turning around, she narrowed the most hateful glare he'd ever seen. Which given the fact that he'd served Nick's father, the Adarian Malachai, said it all. Adarian had never looked at him with anything other than absolute loathing.

He should be used to it. Yet for some reason, it hurt him that Lyseah wore that same disappointed hatred for him.

How pathetic am I? To allow himself to be hurt by the scorn of a woman who'd betrayed him and allowed him to be enslaved.

She curled her lip. "Are you going to speak? Or just stare at me like the idiot you are?"

There was a time when Caleb would have been able to charm the anger out of her. When he could make her smile regardless of her rage or sorrow.

Those days were gone. He was no longer that same vicious demon he'd been then, and she wasn't the young demon who'd forgive him for any transgression.

After everything they'd shared, they were basically strangers.

Worse, they were enemies.

Still, he regretted what had happened. Not that he'd left, but rather what it'd done to her. "I just wanted to say that I never lied to you. When I told you that I loved you, it was the truth."

"But *I* wasn't enough."

Caleb winced at the hurt in her voice. And the truth of that statement. "You were more than enough."

"Then why? Tell me! A *human*!" She spat that word at him. "How could you?"

"Because..." His throat tightened as he remembered the gentleness of Lilliana's touch. The way she'd smiled and held him like no one before.

Or since.

Lyseah had been so different. She'd held him like a grudge. Fierce. Hostile. Resentfully. As if she hated herself for loving him and took it out on him. Her love had been stifling, but it'd been all he'd ever known, and he'd thought it was the best he'd ever know.

Demons didn't love the same way humans did. Or could. Then again, some humans could be every bit as cruel and demeaning. Demanding.

Abusive.

But it wasn't Lyseah's fault. She hadn't known love or tenderness any more than he had. They'd been raised in a place where abuse and love were synonymous. Where any show of weakness was exploited or punished.

Like the Malachai.

"You were more than enough, and I was proud to call you mine."

"Then why did you go with a *human*?"

"You'll never understand." How could she?

"Try me."

Caleb searched his mind for something that would make her understand and give her the answers she was looking for. "She was soft, Seah. Gentle."

"Weak, you mean."

He inclined his head to her. "As I said. You can't understand, and it's not your fault. I didn't understand what it meant to love or be loved until I met her." More than that, he hadn't thought he deserved better.

Violence was all he'd ever known. All he'd expected from everyone.

Sadly, it was all he received.

Until his precious Lil.

Hissing, Lyseah dragged her claws over his neck. "I hate you, Malphas! I wish you'd died in battle!"

"So do I." And he meant those words to the core of his being.

Still, there was no sympathy in her eyes as she motioned to the others to take flight. Without another word, she flew off.

Itzal stayed behind.

Caleb had no idea why. It wasn't exactly in his brother's nature to do so. "Breaking rank, brother?"

Itzal shrugged. "I was never much of a follower. Of all demons, you know that."

Yes, he did. His brother had always been a rebel. Even to the idiot depths of Nick. "I don't want to get you into trouble."

Itzal gave him a lopsided grin that exposed his fangs. "I'm always in trouble."

That was true enough. Or at least it used to be. When they were younger, Itzal had courted trouble like it was the last morsel on Earth and if he didn't have it, he'd starve.

Caleb looked in the direction Lyseah had flown off. "Is she going to tell on us?"

"Probably. As you saw, you're not her friend."

"Awesome." Caleb glanced to Nick before he turned back to face his brother. "Who will she be reporting to?"

"Not Cyprian, if that's what you're asking. He's not here."

Caleb let out a sigh of relief. "Then who's in charge?"

"Mot."

And that sucked all the relief right out of him. Mot was Laguerre's husband, who normally went by the name Grim. Cyprian's psycho stepfather who'd been out to destroy Nick for years.

Crap.

Grim hated Nick passionately. If Grim caught wind of this, he'd be after them with so many reinforcements that they'd blot the light from the sky. No one could stand up to the army he'd throw at them.

"How much time?"

Itzal thought about it for a second. "She's probably in his throne room, right now, telling him about you and the Malachai."

"Should we run?" Nick asked.

"Only if you want to get caught. Anything that runs sets off alarms."

Bubba sheathed his sword. "Then what do you suggest?"

"Prayer?"

Caleb smirked at Nick's automatic response for most things. Mostly because of his mom, who said it could cure anything, quell anything, and give guidance through the darkest night.

"Anything better?" Caleb asked.

Itzal bristled. "I might know something. Maybe."

"Don't play with me, Itzal."

He gave Caleb a smile that resembled the one Nick always tried to use to get himself out of trouble. "What can I say? I like to see you sweat."

Aeron came up and clapped him on the back. "While I respect the fact you like to see your brother sweat, boyo, I'd rather not bleed. What say you find this something before I turn me mates loose on you?" He glanced over to Kaziel. "They love themselves some demon meat."

Fear actually entered Itzal's eyes. "How many of you can fly?"

Caleb looked around their group. "Three of us have wings. Five don't."

Those words caused Xev to flinch. Caleb had forgotten about the fact that his brother's wings had been severed as punishment. It was something that always haunted Xev.

He would apologize for mentioning it, but that would only make it worse.

"Well, that just sucks!" Itzal let out an exaggerated sigh. "Fine. Follow me."

Nick wasn't so sure about this. He cut a curious glance to Xev, who shrugged. *Do you know this guy?* He sent his question silently to Xev.

I do. He was Caleb's second-in-command.

Huh. That was interesting. Again, something Nick should have thought about, but never had. *Did you ever fight him?*

Xev didn't answer at first. Rather, he sent an evil glare toward Itzal. *Want to see the scars? He's the one who turned Caleb in for being with Lilliana.*

Nick stumbled at that. "What the..."

Itzal, Kody, Caleb, and Bubba looked at him.

"Sorry. Tripped. You know me, clumsy Cajun. No idea where my limbs are at any given time."

Once they were on their way again, he glanced sideways at Xev. *Then why are we following him?*

Caleb's an idiot.

While it definitely seemed that way, Nick knew the

truth. Caleb wasn't stupid. Nor was he trusting.

It practically took an act of Congress to get the beast to agree to pizza. Why was he following someone who'd betrayed him?

Caleb? What are you doing?

Keeping my enemies close.

That almost made Nick trip again. *You think he's leading us into a trap?*

No, but I'm assuming it's a trap.

Any particular reason you're leading us there if you suspect he's got something planned?

For the fun of it.

In that moment, Nick wished he was close enough to kick his demon. Walking into a trap wasn't exactly his idea of fun, but Caleb was a different beast.

As Nick ducked to go under a branch, Kody let out a scream.

He turned to see her being cradled by a tree. Literally. The limbs were wrapped around her waist, throat, and arms as it lifted her off her feet.

Nick's nostrils flared. Fury went through him so ferociously that he felt his body shift into his Malachai form. "Let her go!" His voice was low and gravelly.

Without thinking, he rushed toward it, only to have Caleb knock him away.

"Stop. It'll kill her if you attack."

"Seriously?"

"Seriously." Itzal headed toward the tree slowly. Once he was close enough, he began to rub its trunk.

"What are you doing?" 'Cause a lot of things went through Nick's mind, and he didn't want to jump to any conclusions.

"I'm soothing it."

The tree began to droop. Then slowly, it lowered Kody back to the ground.

Nick rushed to her to help her get away. "What was that?"

"We're intruding on their territory," Itzal said. "Don't step on their roots. It offends them."

Nick stepped a bit farther away from the root that was barely an inch from his shoe.

"Wish you'd told me that sooner." Kody rubbed at her wrists as she eyed her captor tree. "Being yanked off my feet offends me. Thinking I should go Paul Bunyan on it and make a bench."

"Would that make me Babe, the big blue ox?" Nick flashed a grin he hoped was charming.

"Nah," Caleb said wryly. "I think it makes Itzal the big orange jackass for not warning us."

Kody and Bubba burst out laughing. Nick chuckled, as he agreed that Itzal was a jackass. "That sounds about right. Anything else we need to avoid, Nemo?"

Caleb screwed his face up. "Uh! Why did you put that image in my brain? Now I can't unsee it."

Nick ignored him as he waited for a response.

Itzal looked at each of them in turn. "All of you think I'm leading you into a trap." He said that as a statement and not a question.

Aeron crossed his arms over his chest. "The thought did come to me mind. Are you?"

"That's what I told Lyseah I'd do." Itzal's gaze went to Caleb. "But I keep thinking back to the day you almost died protecting me."

Caleb sucked his breath in. It was a memory never far from his thoughts. That was the wound that had led him to Lilliana.

Even now, he could see that day so clearly. He'd fallen to the ground and been trying to find some place to hide.

Lil had been picking herbs in the woods when he'd stumbled upon her.

Fear had drained the color from her beautiful face as she saw him. He'd expected her to scream and call for help. To run.

Instead, she'd dropped her gaze to the blood pouring out of his side. "You're hurt."

From the moment she'd touched him to help, it'd shattered the icy organ in his chest that he'd thought had no use other than to pump his cold blood. Even after all these centuries, he could still see the concern in her eyes as she'd helped him to a cave, where she'd tended his wound and brought him food.

Day after day.

The other humans would have killed her had they found out what she was doing. Helping a demon.

She hadn't cared. Nor had she betrayed him. Not once.

Her heart was beyond all reasoning.

Itzal met his gaze. "I owe you, brother. I haven't forgotten. Nor have I forgotten that I'm the reason you betrayed us and were punished over it."

"I should be thanking you."

Itzal snorted. "No. Not the way you were beaten and humiliated. You should hate me for eternity."

Loving Lilliana had never been a punishment. It'd been the only happiness he'd ever known in his excessively long life. Like Xev, he'd gladly endure his torture and more if he could have even a single hour with her, again.

Itzal's gaze returned to Aeron. "So, to answer your question, I'm not betraying you. But it doesn't mean everything around us isn't sending word to your enemies." He shifted his gaze to something over Aeron's shoulder. "Or trying to kill you."

Nick barely had time to duck before Itzal sent a blast from his hands to something behind them. A scream sounded as Nick turned around to see a shadow demon burst apart.

Caleb took it in stride.

Until a loud howl sounded.

Kaziel's ears picked up, then he began to growl.

"Uh, what's that?"

Before anyone could answer Nick's question, a pack of three-headed dogs broke through the underbrush. They were coming straight for them.

When Kaziel started forward, Aeron grabbed his collar. "Not yet, lad. You're outnumbered and likely to bleed."

"Or die." Vawn began shooting more god-bolts at them.

Nick used his powers to conjure fire. He shot them at the dogs. It barely slowed them down and did no real damage. Dang it all. "How do we kill these things?"

Caleb put up a shield to hold them back. "You don't."

Itzal agreed. "Cut off a head and three more grow back. They shoot fire and have the most lethal venom you can imagine. One bite... you're dead."

"Yeehaw! Venomous hellhounds. Just what I wanted for a pet." Nick rubbed at his chin. "Ideas? Anyone?"

"Throw our shoes at them and hope they chase

them?"

Nick passed a droll stare to Xev for that suggestion.

"I do cat things when I'm a cat that I don't want to. Natural instinct. They might actually act like dogs."

That was a thought.

Nick took a shoe off and threw it. Sadly, it hit Caleb's shield wall, rebounded, and hit him in the head. "You suck, *grand-père*. Anyone else have a stupid idea?"

Caleb shook his head. "I expended all my stupidity when I followed you here. And at the expense of being a massive downer, they're burning through my shield. I won't be able to hold them back much longer."

Sweat gathered on Nick's forehead as he watched them snarling and drooling venom.

Then he froze as an idea occurred to him. It was about as stupid as throwing his shoe, but...

Better than nothing.

Moving away from his friends, he went full Malachai. Bad breath. Big black wings and horns. Red and black mottled skin with glowing red eyes. The whole boudin.

The only thing was that he wished he was this muscled and tall as a human. In Malachai form, he was ripped like Rambo, and seven feet all, not the scrawny teen who stared back at him in a mirror with eyes full of self-loathing.

Intimidating, indeed. Extending his wings, he approached the dogs that continued to try and break through the shield. Nick exposed his fangs, then let out a loud war cry that rivaled one of Vawn's screams.

The hellhounds yelped and started backing away.

Nick stepped forward and let out another bellow. Whining like pups, the dogs ran off.

"That's right! I'm the head demon. Bow before me. I don't need a shoe to throw at you, Scooby!" Nick pounded his chest, then turned to see Kody staring at him with an arched brow.

"Feeling proud, are you?"

Nick postured. "C'mon. Admit it. I make this look sexy."

She shook her head. "While I admit you are one of the best-looking guys I've ever known, no one can make your Malachai form look good. Kind of the way Caleb loses a lot of appeal when he goes Nemo."

"Hey!"

"Sorry. It's true. Your demon form leaves a lot to be desired."

"I'll give her that," Vawn agreed. "The red and orange do clash, Malphas."

Nick felt his form fading. "Y'all so mean. Why you want to hurt me like that, *cher*?"

She gave him a quick kiss. "You're still my hero."

That helped. A little, at least. Nick put his arm around her as he looked to Itzal. "So, what's going to try and eat us next?"

"No telling. Keep your eyes open and your tones low."

"My tone?"

"Voice!"

Oh. That made sense. And once again, Nick felt like an idiot.

Kody laced her fingers with his as they returned to following after Itzal.

But as they walked, Nick couldn't shake the feeling that they were being watched.

And followed.

The sensation crawled over his skin and made the hair at the nape of his neck rise. Worse was the feeling that the dogs were still on their heels.

His Malachai senses were buzzing.

He had no idea why until they topped the next hill. The clouds overhead began rolling in like a living being. It brought with it a heavy fog.

"What's going on?"

Itzal held his hand up to silence them, which made Nick's hackles rise even higher.

"They know we're here."

6

Without warning and with no discernible target, Itzal sliced at the shadows all around them.

Nick scowled. What the heck? Did he have some form of demon Parvo? Would make sense, given his frenetic attacks against nothing. "What's he doing?"

"Shadow demons." Bubba began slashing at the shadows, too.

Nick's frown deepened. They kept using that term, and it took him a minute to figure out what they were actually facing, and why they were attacking them so viciously.

"You mean a shadowalker?"

Itzal nodded.

Nick's heart stopped. They were one of the worst

class of demons that straddled two worlds. With no loyalty whatsoever to anyone or anything. Morally ambiguous and capricious in the purest sense of those words, they were as likely to kill someone as to help them.

But they weren't usually found in this desolate place.

"How?" Nick asked.

Itzal gave him an irritated grimace. "Those who once oversaw and policed them are no longer here to wrangle them."

Shadow... He must have been neutralized, too. Made sense as he was one of Ambrose's best friends. Without him around to guard the shadow realm and keep it solid, the walls must have collapsed.

Dang. Out of control, morally ambiguous demons. Just what they needed.

The shadows moved over them, causing a harsh and horrible pain. Nick's skin felt as if it were on fire, and that the fire was burning him all the way to his bones.

Kaziel howled. Aeron cursed as he did his best to battle them, too.

Nick had no idea how to fight them. How to stop the pain that kept getting worse. He might be a Malachai, but they could be wounded and severely hurt.

Neutralized.

Kody groaned in agony.

Nick crawled toward her so that he could help. No matter what, he had to keep her safe.

Just as he reached her, she pulled out her mother's sword. Like a lightsaber, the metal glowed so bright that it lit up the entire area around her.

And them.

He held his hand up to shield his eyes as the demons screamed and withdrew.

"Light..." Of course. They were shadows. Bright light would drive them away. It made sense that they wouldn't be able to attack them in bright light.

I should have thought of that, especially given how dark it's become.

But Kody was smarter than he was, and he knew it. Not to mention the fact that she'd probably battled them in her past.

Caleb stood up first. "Everyone okay?"

"No. Kaziel's hurt bad." Vawn held a cloth to Kaziel's side. It was already saturated with blood.

Itzal didn't move.

Caleb went to his brother. "Itzzy?"

Itzal blinked slowly. "Did we survive?"

Nick met Caleb's tormented gaze. He didn't know what to say. Their group was mostly okay. Itzal not so much.

As if he knew how dire his situation was, Itzal

looked down at his wounds. "Oh. That's not good."

"Don't talk." Caleb glanced around their group.

For all their collective powers, none of them had the ones that could heal.

Or save the demon's life.

Itzal grimaced. "You have to get to Noir's castle. What you're looking for is in the back garden, protected by Noir's pet. You can sneak in and…" His voice trailed off as his eyes turned dull.

"Itzzy?" Caleb shook him gently. "Itzzy, talk to me. Don't you dare die like this!"

But it was too late. He was gone.

Nick didn't know what to do. He'd never seen Caleb distraught. Pissed, check. Grumpy, double check. Happy, rarely. But grief…

The closest he'd seen was the sadness that darkened his eyes whenever he spoke of his wife.

Kneeling down, Nick reached to touch his shoulder. "I'm sorry, Cay."

Caleb continued to hold his brother. "It's all my fault. We shouldn't have come here."

"We had no choice."

Tears misted in Caleb's serpent eyes, but he refused to let them fall. "We had a choice. Why are we trying to save a world that has never shown mercy to any of us? Why not let Cyprian burn it to the ground?"

He wasn't wrong. That was the hardest part about swallowing all this, and Nick struggled to find words that might comfort him. Sadly, he wasn't good at these kinds of pep talks. That was why the good Lord had given him his mom and Kody. They knew how to soothe and comfort.

His knack was for saying the wrong thing at the worst possible time. Hoof-in-mouth-itis. That was his disease.

But this was his responsibility. "Itzal was with us, trying to prevent that. I know you don't want him to have died in vain."

Caleb curled his lip, and in that moment, Nick saw the ferocious demon lord who'd once led an army. "What do I care about any of this?"

He had no answer for that. Caleb had been done wrong by so many. The world was harsh, and it was cold.

Nick wasn't even sure why *he* cared.

Vawn cleared his throat. "Nick?"

He looked over his shoulder. "How's Kaziel doing?"

"Still alive, but I think he's out for the count. He needs to rest and heal."

Caleb might be in the same condition, too. Honestly, Nick didn't have a whole lot of fight left in him, either. It seemed like that was all they'd been doing. Fighting to the bitter end.

He missed having down time.

Being a student who knew nothing of all this.

Curse you, Kyrian.

Had Kyrian not saved him, Nick would have known nothing of the Dark-Hunters.

Would it matter?

He would have still become the Malachai.

Or would he?

In all known versions of his life, his father had been alive when Nick had first met Kyrian. At that fateful meeting, Nick had been stabbed in the original timeline and then shot after Ambrose had tampered with their lives.

Either way, shot or stabbed, had Kyrian not been there to take him to the hospital, his wounds would have killed him. There would have been no Acheron. No Dark-Hunters.

No Malachai because his father would have continued on in that role.

Maybe that would have been for the best. Adarian had seemed content to wait for his mom to love him in return and to welcome him into her life.

It would only have lasted until she died. Or Adarian grew tired of her. Then again, there was no telling what Adarian might have done to her once he was through. If he had grown bored, he was just as likely to kill her as not.

Not that any of that really mattered had Nick died.

Anything happens to you, Nicky, they'll have to dig two graves.

No. His mom wouldn't have survived his death. One way or another, she'd have died, too. Which meant his father wouldn't have stayed in New Orleans. He'd have returned to being a bloodthirsty beast out to end the world.

By saving his life, Kyrian had unknowingly saved everyone else.

Except his mother who'd died a decade later because Nick had entered the world of the Dark-Hunters.

You can't go back. You know that.

Would have. Should have. Could have.

Whatever was past was done. There was no way to change it. Ambrose had proven that.

Like it or not, this was their future, and he was in control here. Not that it felt like he was in control of anything. Life just kept hitting him in the crotch when he wasn't looking.

You are the Malachai.

But he sure didn't feel like one, and maybe that was

the problem. His powers scared him. There was so much that he still didn't know.

Other than he was destined to end the world by fathering a son who hated him.

No. He *was* evil. To his bitter core.

For that reason alone, he had to maintain control and keep the demon inside him leashed. Otherwise, he'd be no better than Cyprian. Better his son destroy the world than he do it himself.

Staring over the devastation, he sighed. "Vawn, you and Caleb stay here with Aeron."

"What?"

"No!"

"Forget it, mate!"

Nick held a hand up to stop their protests. "I have Kody, Xev, and Bubba. Y'all need a few to lick and tend your wounds. We can handle this. Stay here and we'll be back for you."

Kody bit her lip. "I don't know, Nick..."

"It'll be fine," Nick assured her. "I have no doubt about our success."

Xev cleared his throat. "For the record, I do. I have tons and tons of doubt. Enough for all of us."

Honestly, so did Nick. And it didn't help that two of their party were dead or wounded. The last thing he wanted was to lose anyone else.

He clapped Xev on the arm. "C'mon, *grand-père*. We can handle this."

"I'm glad you have found your confidence again. Just wish it wasn't right now." Xev followed reluctantly.

Nick didn't respond as he dug through his inherited memories to find a map of this place. All of his predecessors had been here in this dismal domain at one time or another. His father had called it home for centuries.

In Adarian's case, it wasn't by choice. He'd been held captive here. It was part of what had driven him insane. A Malachai never did well in captivity. They would cut off their own limbs to escape. Kill any and every single one they could. There were just some beasts it didn't pay to capture.

And as Nick was tripping through those memories, he saw one of Xev.

It was so stunning that he almost stopped walking. "You visited my father here?"

Xev nodded. "Many times."

Because his father had bartered Xev's blood to other demons and even to his overlords.

Their abuse of Xev was biblical.

"No wonder you hated me when we first met."

Xev's harsh gaze softened. "To be fair, I didn't know we were related."

That was the least of it, and Nick doubted it would

have mattered, given the severity of Xev's treatment. He'd been afraid Nick was as evil as those who'd come before him.

Good bet, actually. Nick could feel that evil coursing through his veins with every beat of his heart.

But he'd never treated Xev or anyone else the way his father had. He refused to let those genes win. Instead, Nick had freed him from the hell that had been his punishment.

"I'm sorry for everything previous Malachais did to you."

"Not your fault."

Xev might say that, but Nick knew the sadness Xev felt. It resonated inside him. Like Caleb and Bubba, Xev had paid a harsh price for being loved.

No one should ever be punished because they'd loved someone.

Nick's heart broke over that. People like him took for granted the love in their lives. He'd never had to pay a price. His mother's love was unconditional and eternal.

As was Kody's.

They had never charged him for it or asked anything more than for him to love them back. Caleb and Xev had been forced to hide their love. To let no one know for fear of losing everything.

In the end, they'd lost it anyway, and paid for that love with their blood and souls.

I'm so lucky.

At least he knew it. He didn't take for granted the people in his life who would die for him. The people who valued him more than themselves.

Yeah, it might suck to be the Malachai, but unlike those before him, he had a family.

That was what life was all about. Finding those who could be depended on when it mattered most. Those who didn't flinch when things were hard or when someone wasn't perfect.

The ones who would stand by your side to the end of the world.

And beyond.

Bubba drew up short. "What's that sound?"

"My heartbeat?"

He narrowed his gaze at Nick. "Do you not hear it?"

Nick struggled, but all he heard were the voices in his head, calling him names and telling him that he was a disappointment to everyone and everything.

The color faded from Xev's face as he moved to cover Kody. "It's the seeds of doubt."

Nick scowled at something he'd never heard of before. "What?"

Xev put a finger in his ear to clear it. "It's one of the

protections here. Demons who look inside your heart and whisper to you about your greatest fears and failures."

Nick groaned out loud. "Oh, great. I have enough of this inside my head. Really don't need anything adding to the screaming doubts I already have."

"Keep saying that. If they take root inside you, they'll paralyze you with fear and will eat away at your soul."

"Oh, even better! They're piranha demons. Like the world really needs that. So, how do we kill them, *grand-père*?"

"Can't. They're immortal and insidious."

"Nothing's really immortal. Everything can be killed," Nick reminded Xev.

"Not these. They really are immortal and eternal. All you can do is fight them off."

"With what?"

"Confidence. You can't believe them. Just keep repeating, 'I'm the best me possible. I'm enough and I'm worthy. I will rise.'"

Nick held his hand out to Kody. "I can't do that alone and believe it."

"Me, either." She took his hand. "And for the record, you are enough. I think you're perfect and wonderful."

Those words tightened his throat. More grateful for her than he could ever express, he kissed her hand that was entwined with his. "You are the best woman in all the world. No one is a greater warrior or girlfriend. You're so perfect, you make perfect weep."

Kody smiled.

"I'm going to be sick." Xev made retching sounds.

Nick scoffed at his teasing. "So, what are you saying to yourself, *grand-père*?"

"I'm not dead yet."

Bubba laughed at Xev's surly words. "I think I'll make that my mantra."

Nick arched a brow. "I thought yours was *come get some*."

"It was, but I think I prefer Xev's."

Kody tightened the grip on Nick's hand.

"You all right, *cher*?"

"They're telling me that I failed you and my parents and brothers. That I failed everyone."

Nick shook his head. "You have *never* failed me. You couldn't."

"But I did, Nick. I know I did. I went down and wasn't there to protect your back."

He stopped and turned her to face him. "Look at me, Kody. Don't let them in your head. You have failed no one."

Bubba stumbled.

"Big guy?"

He caught himself. "I'm fine, kid. If I survived Mark's insults for all those years, I can do this. Trust me, they're amateurs."

Nick glanced to Xev. "What about you?"

"They're bringing up things I'd really like to forget. But I was raised under my mother's scalding tongue. Like Bubba said, they're amateurs compared to Azura."

Given that Nick had memories of Xev's mother laying into his father over nothing, he could only imagine the horrific things she'd said to her son. That harsh beast didn't have a single kind word for anyone.

Now, she was unleashed into the world of man.

Yeah. They needed to get a handle on this.

You're worthless. How can you get a handle on anything? Everything you touch, you screw up. You should have died at birth. You destroy everyone and everything you come into contact with.

Your mother would be alive had you not been her son.

Nick staggered as those demons laid into him.

Why are you alive when so many good people have died? Your father died to save you, and what have you done with your life? Nothing.

You're worthless from your first breath to your last. Do the world a favor and end it all.

"Umph!" Nick winced as they kept belting him with

everything he already thought when it came to his existence.

"You okay, bud?"

He nodded at Bubba. "Remember, I went to school with Stone Blakemore. He said worse things to me on a daily basis."

Because he was right. He saw just what a loser you are. Why should anyone fight for you? You're a betrayer. A failure.

All you do is take. When was the last time you gave anything to anyone?

Nick growled in defiance. "Now that last one just isn't true. Call me worthless all you want, and I'll agree. But I'm not selfish. Never have, never will be that! I've taken care of my mother every day of my life!" he shouted at the demons. "I watch over my friends, and I take care of my girl. So sod off, you losers. Find someone else to lie to." He felt his Malachai fangs drop down. "You want to pick on someone? C'mon. I dare you!"

Something akin to a sonic boom went through him, then it spread out in a circle around them.

Feral screams filled the air. Nick felt his eyes change and with that, he was able to see them.

Tiny, insignificant beasts, they were twisted and hideous. Soulless. When he started toward them, they shrank away— too terrified to face him, knowing the lies they'd spoken.

Nick shook his head at them. "You insult us? You're nothing but soul-sucking animals. Take your hate and lies, and get out before I set you on fire!"

Then again, he *was* the Malachai. That was something he could do easily. Nick let out a blast of fire and listened as they screamed in agony.

He tsked at them. "You're the ones who made nothing of your lives. You spread hatred and pick on those who are weak, where they're weakest. Any mongrel can do that. It takes someone special to build others up instead of tearing them down."

Nick turned to Kody. She was such a special being. When he was weakest, she, like his mom, reached out to save him. No hesitation. No questions. They guided those who were lost and unable to see the goodness inside themselves into a safe harbor.

They spread light through the darkest storms. Not for any reason other than it was the right thing to do.

His breathing ragged, Nick watched as the soulless demons burned to ashes. Then the wind caught them and blew them into oblivion.

If only real doubt was so easy to cast off.

"What did you do?" Xev asked.

"What I had to. No one attacks my family and gets away with it."

Kody approached him slowly. "Nick?"

It was only then that he realized he was in full Malachai form. But he was still himself.

For once, there was no hatred or violence demanding release. The Malachai wasn't salivating for blood or trying to take him over. Nick turned his black and red hands over as he studied them. "How can I still be me?"

Xev took his hand. "Because this *is* you. You are the Malachai."

That touch made his memories surge as he reconciled the man he wanted to be and the monster he'd been born.

He saw his ancestors from thousands of years ago.

Monakribos... Apollymi's son. The Malachai who'd started this curse because they'd taken everything from him.

He was standing beside Xev. They were young in appearance. Boys who were playing in an open field. Laughing in a way Nick had never known Xev to laugh.

The two of them were shooting bolts of light into the darkening sky. It fell back toward them as sparks that reminded him of soundless fireworks.

Xev flew off and Monakribos chased him.

"You can't catch me, cuz! I'm faster!"

His wings flapping frenetically, Xev grabbed his foot. "Say that again."

"I'm taking it easy on you, old demon. I don't want to show you up with my awesomeness."

Nick was amazed at the beauty of Xev's face. He'd never known this side of him. Too much had happened to steal that joy away.

Just as it'd stolen Monakribos's sanity.

Why? Did life really have to be so harsh?

"Nick?"

The sound of Xev's voice jolted him back to the present.

"Where were you?"

Blinking, Nick glanced at the three of them. "You were friends with Monakribos."

"I was."

"He wasn't always a demon, craving blood." For some reason, Nick had never thought about that. In all the memories he'd seen in the past, Monakribos had been a fierce warrior. Always stern and somber.

Sadness darkened Xev's eyes. "We're all kids in the beginning. Innocent and trusting. Until life kicks it out of us."

Funny, he'd never really thought about that.

"But," Xev said softly, "we were still born demons."

That didn't matter. Not every demon was evil.

And Nick finally understood what everyone had been trying to tell him. "I don't have to be a destroyer."

Kody reached up to cup his face in her hands. "You choose your fate, Boo. Don't let others turn you into something you're not. You be you, always."

Tears misted Xev's eyes at those words. "She's right. I allowed the hate of my parents to turn me into a tool for their insanity. I did what I thought I'd been born for, until I met Myone. She gave me the freedom to be the creature I chose. To find my own way."

Now, Nick had finally found his.

"I'm the Malachai."

"And you're still Nick."

How simple, really. Yet he'd been so busy trying to avoid his destiny that he'd never taken a moment to understand what he was running from. What being the Malachai really meant.

I have a choice.

For better or worse. He controlled his destiny, not some unwritten prophecy made up hundreds of thousands of years ago, and retold as a story to frighten kids.

He was in control.

"Do you think we can make Cyprian understand that he doesn't have to be a destroyer? That he can be more?"

If they could get his son to stop hating... To embrace his fate without the fury and baggage of their pasts...

Maybe they could save him.

"I don't know." Bubba glanced over to Kody. "Sometimes people go too far and can't come back from it."

"We can try." Kody smiled at him. "That's all anyone can do."

And that was why Nick loved her so much. Her positivity that was so rare. It was easy to see the bad and to tear things down. It took someone special to see the good and to build someone up, regardless of what was going on in their own life.

Speak the truth. People suck. They're not worth saving.

Nick hissed as he stepped back from them to see the demon that was trying to torment him. "Missed one." He started to blast it, then paused.

"Get over here." He did a perfect *Mortal Kombat* move and yanked the demon to his side. "Do you know who I am?"

It blinked its clear eyes at him. Being a shadow, its twisted form made it appear like a crooked, translucent stick. "You're the Malachai."

"You know what I can do to you?"

It nodded.

"Then why did you come at me, dude? Seriously?"

"That's what I do."

The scorpion and the frog. An easy excuse. *It's my nature, so whatever I do is okay.*

Yet I'm nothing special. Nick refused to follow the cycle he'd been born into. *If I can break my fate and create a new destiny, what's your excuse?*

There wasn't one. And he wasn't about to let this demon get away with lying and not accepting responsibility for its actions.

"Maybe you ought to learn a new hobby, huh? Get out and party with some friends. Do something constructive."

"Are you going to kill me?"

It was tempting. Really, really tempting… Okay, so the Malachai in him wasn't completely tamed. It was salivating for a taste of stupid demon.

But Nick held it back. "You going to give me a reason to kill you?"

"I'd rather not."

"Then you can live. Go do something good and stop being nasty."

Nodding, the demon rushed away so fast that it stumbled, pushed itself up, and ran off into the woods.

"What just happened?" Xev asked.

Nick winced. "Yeah, I forgot y'all can't see them. I just sent one of those runts off."

"You didn't kill him?"

"Nope."

Xev tsked. "Then you're a better demon than I am. I wouldn't have resisted."

"Thank you, *grand-père*." Nick kissed him on the cheek.

Normally, Xev would have shoved him.

This time, he pulled Nick into a hug and kissed the top of his head. "You're right, kudzu. You do grow on people."

"And that's how you get sucked in." Bubba sighed. "I tried to kick him out of my store when he was a kid, but he just kept coming back until I finally gave up and welcomed the evil in."

Laughing, Nick started toward the fortress they needed to reach. Yet as he walked, he had a weird feeling.

They weren't alone. Something else was stalking them. He just couldn't figure out what.

"WHAT DO you want us to do?"

Grim sat on Noir's old throne that was made of bones from the demons Noir had slaughtered for pleasure, as he considered that question.

The multicolored demons around him were supposed to be the best of his army.

How pathetic. It was a wonder they'd defeated the humans.

Or even a mouse.

Was this really all there was?

Best of the best, my ass.

"My lord?"

Still, he ignored the demon in front of him. He should probably notify Laguerre that the Malachai was in their domain.

Then again, he was in no mood for her tantrums. Or that of her son. Cyprian had way too much of her personality for his liking or tolerance.

Cold and biting. He could do without that brat.

He was a death god. One who'd helped train Nick Gautier. *I can handle this.*

I can handle them.

Rising to his feet, he moved away from the throne. The walls around him flickered with images of the small group that was heading toward them. Funny how Azura and Noir once used this to keep an eye on their dark domain and the world above. Now, he seldom looked at it. He didn't care what others did as a rule. Not unless they ventured onto his lands or into his private space...

like this little group that was agitating him with their trespass.

And in spite of his name, he much preferred the bright light that kept his enemies from hiding in the shadows.

He had plans for them...

Summoning his armor, he left to confront the interlopers.

CYPRIAN FROZE instantly as a weird sensation went through him. "Mother?" The name was out of his mouth before he could stop it.

Much to his chagrin.

She stopped in the doorway he'd been headed for, then turned to give him an irritated smirk. "What is your problem now?"

"Lack of maternal care and affection. No positive male role model, and a need for blood that was bred into me before I was born. But that's not why I called you."

His sneered diatribe succeeded in angering her more. "Really? You think I care?"

No. He knew she didn't. That was part of his problem. She cared for nothing and no one.

Only power.

Her reputation. And she'd destroy anyone who threatened either of her two loves.

So he returned her disgust with his own. "I think you'll care about this."

"Doubtful." She returned to his side in a huff. "And I better care."

He rolled his eyes. "What if I told you that I just had a shift in my memory?"

"A what?"

Cyprian cocked his head as a wave of dizziness went through him. "My memories are changing."

"You idiot. That's called remembering something you've forgotten."

He wasn't the idiot. She was. "No, Mum. I would have remembered my father meeting with his friends in the future to kill me. That's not something one forgets easily."

The smugness left her features as they settled into a shocked expression. "What?"

"Exactly. They're trying to stop us and as they do so, they're letting me know."

"How is that possible?"

He shrugged. "I guess it has to do with our shared memories. When he creates a new one, it comes to me automatically."

Laguerre actually laughed at that. "This is beautiful! By trying to stop you, he's helping you to stop him. I love that irony."

He loved stupidity. And the fact that his father was so trusting.

"It gets better, Mum. I know exactly what they're doing. We're not only going to stop them... he's making me even stronger in the process."

7

"Uncle Ambrose?"

Nick froze at the unfamiliar voice. Scowling, he turned around slowly until he faced a beautiful blonde teenager.

With red eyes.

What the...?

"Hello?" he asked hesitantly.

Relief poured over her features as she ran toward him and threw herself into his arms. "I knew you weren't dead! No one believed me, but I knew. You're stronger than that. There's no way anyone could defeat you! Especially not a knock-off Malachai."

Gaping, he looked at Kody. "Uh... who is this?"

Kody laughed. "She's Xenia."

That caused the girl to stiffen in his embrace. Her

gaze narrowing, she stepped back to confront Kody. "Who are you?"

"Nyria."

Her scowl deepened. "Aunt Nyria's older than you are."

"I know. It's a long story, Xen. Suffice it to say that Ambrose and I are back from the past. We've come to free Uncle Acheron."

"You can't..." Her voice trailed off as she saw Xev. "Uncle XeXe?"

He glanced at Kody. "Maybe?"

Laughing, the little sprite went to hug him, too. "I never thought I'd see you again! Oh! I'm so happy you're here."

Who is she? he mouthed over her shoulder to Kody.

"She's Thorn's youngest daughter."

Xev gaped. "Thorn has another child?"

"Yep."

Xenia pulled back to look up at him with a frown. "You don't know me?"

"He's a past Xev. Not your current uncle."

Confusion played across her adorable face until her features lifted and she smiled. "Oh... That's what Mom meant. I should have known."

"Mom?" Nick asked.

Kody quickly made sounds to shush them. "No one

needs to know that information. I probably shouldn't have even mentioned she was Thorn's. But if you know more than that, you could seriously mess up the future and jeopardize her birth."

"Don't do that." Xenia appeared horrified by the mere thought. "I have to be here. And I want to be born."

"Why?" Bubba asked.

Something whistled.

Xenia's eyes widened. "We have to go. Grim is heading this way. We don't want him to find us."

Before Nick could ask more, she disappeared into the woods.

He and the others followed while he tried to make sense of this. Thorn had a daughter...

It shouldn't seem as impossible as it did. After all, he had a son. Why couldn't he have another kid or two?

'Course Thorn's son had been born thousands of years ago. And Thorn had abandoned that son for centuries to basically a hell realm.

So given that, Nick just couldn't wrap his head around someone as cold and vicious as Thorn having a little girl. Not that Xenia was little now, but she'd have been little at some point.

It totally messed with his head.

And as they made their way through the forest, he

noticed that everything cut a path for Xenia and then closed the path behind them.

"What's up with the trees and plants?"

Xenia cast a grin at him over her shoulder. "They're my family. They'll always protect me."

Good to know.

But he was curious. "Why?"

"Dad brought me here when the fighting in the mortal realm got bad. He wanted to make sure that I stayed safe."

Well that made sense... not at all. Sure. Throw one kid to the demons and protect the other one.

Nick lost a lot of respect for Thorn on that one. How could he be so callous to his son?

"It was Cadegan's idea," Xenia said as if she knew his thoughts. "He was aware that the creatures here had made a pact with our father. So, he talked Dad into giving me ownership of his Azmodean home to keep the others from harming me."

Well, that made him feel a lot better about Thorn. So, the worm had freed his son. "Cadegan got out of his prison? How? When?"

"You heard nothing," Kody cut in. "Xenia, please stop telling Nick about a future he has yet to live. He's from Ambrose's distant past, and we can't let him know what's happened or he might screw everything up."

"Oh." She flashed a smile at them. "Nice scenery, isn't it?"

"Mind-blowing." Nick stepped around her as she held what appeared to be a shrub gate open for them.

After he entered the area, he pulled up short.

Thorn's dismal hall. Only it didn't look so forbidding in the light. It was still painted black and stood out against the landscape, but...

The hall actually looked inviting. Warm. Dare he say, homey?

How weird.

Once they were through the gate, Xenia sealed them in.

"Are they still coming?" Bubba asked.

"Yes, but don't worry. They can't get in here." She wrinkled her nose. "It drives Grim crazy. He thought he'd have this area, too."

"Why doesn't he?" Xev asked.

"The boundary my grandfather set up to protect my dad. Nothing can cross it so long as they mean harm to anyone who's in here."

"You sure?"

She smiled at Nick's question. "While my father and grandfather were forever fighting, I can assure you that my grandpa would never allow anyone to harm my dad, or me."

It weirded him out to hear someone defend Noir. "You spend a lot of time with your grandfather?"

"Not really. My mom hated him with a pink-purple passion, so I wasn't allowed near him."

Nick was desperate to know what had happened to Thorn, especially when they entered the mansion that had belonged to the prickly demigod. But Kody was right. The more he knew, the more dangerous it was. "You live here alone?"

Sadness darkened her eyes. Without comment, she headed toward a mirror on the wall.

Only it wasn't a mirror. When Nick moved closer, he saw a faint image of a man he remembered and a woman he'd never seen before.

"Cadegan and his wife were locked into this by one of Laguerre's hench-demons. I brought it here, and I suspect that they can hear and see everything that goes on in this realm, but I have no way of knowing for sure." She reached up to touch her brother's face. "All I know is that I miss him."

"Can't you get him out?"

She shook her head at Nick. "Acheron or my father could release him, I'm sure, but me..."

Kody patted her arm sympathetically. "That's why we're here. We want to free Acheron."

Nick expected Kody's words to relieve her. Instead, Xenia stared at her in horror. "It's impossible."

"It can't be," he said.

Xenia's eyes filled with tears. "Believe me, I've tried everything I could think of. Nothing's worked. Cyprian turned him to stone and then gifted him to my grandfather. He's kept in a garden that's guarded by Cyprian's pet attack dragon."

Nick gaped. "That's not fair. How did he get an attack dragon? I want one!"

Xenia smirked. "He captured a Were-Hunter and spelled it so that it can't change into a human. Makes for one pissed-off dragon who would give anything to kill Cyprian."

"So, if we befriend the dragon, he'll let us through?"

Xenia rolled her eyes at Nick's hopeful question. "It's not that simple."

"Have you tried?"

"No, but—"

"But nothing. I say we try." Nick looked at the others for corroboration.

Kody folded her arms over her chest. "Don't argue, Xen. You can't win. Believe me, I've tilted that Malachai many a day until my head is sore just from the mere thought of trying to argue him down. Let him try. He often surprises me."

"In a good way, right?" Xenia asked.

Kody slid her gaze to Nick and laughed. "Sometimes."

"Hey, *cher*. I'm not that bad."

"No, but you are *that* stubborn."

He'd argue with her, but sadly, it was the truth. "Can we get to the statue?"

Xen hesitated. "Maybe. We'll have to be careful."

Xev sighed. "What soul-sucking demons are between here and there?"

"Do you really want me to run the catalogue of everything we might face?"

Xev and Bubba exchanged a disgusted grimace. "What do you say, Bubba? Should we just be surprised?"

Bubba sighed. "I like it. Add some spice to our already screwed-up lives. Why not?"

Kody shook her head. "I don't like walking blindly into danger. Other than the dragon who may or may not be befriended, is there anything else on an epic scale we need to be on guard against?"

Xenia counted them off on her fingers. "Man-eating plants. Murder holes. Demons... The list is actually rather long. How much time do we have?"

"Goody!" Nick rubbed his hands together. "Let the insanity begin!"

Kody released a pained groan as they headed for the door.

Nick didn't say much. Rather, he was grateful to have Xev and Bubba with him. Not so much Kody. He'd have preferred that she'd stayed behind where it was safer. He hated putting her in danger.

But what choice did they have?

At least he knew she could take care of herself. God knew she'd pulled his fat out of the fryer enough times to prove she was actually better at hand-to-hand than he was.

'Course his Malachai powers made a mockery of hers, and that was what concerned him. Cyprian wouldn't pull back. He'd have no problem beating her down with everything he had.

Even now, Nick could see her dying on the battle-field. It was enough to bring him to his knees. No one deserved to lose the person they loved.

They dang sure didn't deserve to watch them die in their arms.

I wish I could purge these memories. They were horri-ble, and he didn't want to see them anymore.

He should have burned the Eye, or buried it.

But why show him the future or create the Eye if he couldn't do anything to make it change?

Yeah, that made more sense.

Nick had to believe that he was in control. Not fate. Or destiny or anything else.

He'd already defied all odds. He was a Malachai with morality. One capable of love.

Surely changing the future would be easier than *that*.

Closing his eyes, he remembered the tattoo his friend Tabitha had. *Fate is what we make.*

No one controls me, Nick. Not my parents, my boyfriend, and never destiny. The Fates can kiss my ass.

And that was how she lived. Fearlessly.

He flinched as an image of Tabitha's death haunted him. Everyone had died fighting Cyprian.

I will change this. Or like them, he'd die trying.

Those thoughts stayed in his mind as Xenia led them. "Question?"

She looked at him over her shoulder. "Yeah?"

"Wouldn't it be easier to teleport there?"

Xenia laughed, then stopped. "Oh, you're serious. You meant that."

"Yeah."

"If you want to teleport, I won't stop you. Just remember that anything that lands in my grandfather's home without his permission is immediately imprisoned. And that prison is not a pleasant place. At all." She squinted at him. "It's also Malachai proof."

"But if he's not here..."

"His wards still stand. I could teleport and I'd be fine. It wouldn't be a banner day for any of you if you tried. Still want to chance it?"

Xev cleared his throat. "Having been a POW held by Noir, I don't recommend it. I still have nightmares, and remember that his significant other is my mom. She was worse on me than he was."

Yeah. Nick had seen enough of Azura in the memories of his ancestors that he wanted no part of her. He well understood Xev's hatred.

"Hoofing it is."

Yet it seemed like an endless journey through a haunted wasteland. Yes, there was vegetation. However, it was all twisted and strange. Kind of like a video game. But not nearly as much fun.

"Behold," Nick said in a gravelly voice. "You're on a quest with your fellow adventurers. Bubba, the big giant demon slayer. Xev the house kitty, sucker of your dreams of freedom and perpetual pain in the rump. Kody the magnificent, guardian of your ego, and inspiration to all. And lastly, Xenia, the newbie tracker who—"

"What are you babbling on about?"

Nick grinned at Xenia. "Just passing a good time, *cher*. Trying to keep our spirits up."

Bubba snorted. "Rather you keep your head low and not attract attention to us."

"And that's probably the more intelligent way to go. But the one thing you all know about me, Bubba— I'm braver than I am smart."

"You're proud of this?" Xenia asked.

"I was 'til you took that tone." Nick cleared his throat. "Xenia, crusher of ego, and slayer of Nick's positive attitude."

Before she could respond, a loud screech ripped through the air.

Nick ducked out of habit. "What the heck?"

"It's the trees. They're letting the others know that we're invading."

He wasn't sure what to think about that. "How? How can they make that noise?"

"The wind moving through their leaves."

Bubba glanced around. "Who are they reporting us to?"

"Most likely Grim." She sounded so incredibly perky as she said that. It really was ego-deflating.

How could she sound so chipper about such things?

Xev glanced around. "I'm going to play Nick here for a moment and say that I don't like the sounds of *most likely*. Who else could be around for them to summon?"

Xenia shrugged. "The dragon. Any number of

demons. They could even be signaling Azura, Cyprian, or Noir. But most likely, it's Grim."

Nick stopped to stare at her. "You're remarkably nonchalant, happy and, well, happy about all this. Should I ask why?"

"I prefer not to worry about things until they happen."

"That's crazy!" Nick couldn't believe her laissez-faire attitude. "You need to prepare."

"Why? If it doesn't happen, I'll have wasted all that time that I spent fretting. And no matter how much I worry and plan, whatever happens will be something I never thought of, anyway. Haven't you ever noticed? It's always the thing you didn't think of or see coming that hits you. Not the things you worry about or plan for."

Nick opened his mouth to argue, then stopped.

Crap. She was right. It was always the weird thing he never thought of that brought him to his knees. Life never hit him with the things he worried about.

"Well... anyone else have anything they want to add?" he asked.

"We start cutting down trees so that they can't tell on us?"

Nick laughed at Bubba's suggestion. "I like where your head is, but I don't think we have time for all that."

"Pity."

He agreed, but all they could do was be like Xenia, head forward and hope for a miracle.

It seemed to take forever before they came up to a massive stone wall. Like a sheer mountainside, it rose so high that Nick could barely see the top. Smooth as glass, there was no way to scale it.

"How do we get through this?"

Xenia touched the gray mortar. It shimmered.

What the...

"Remember, my grandfather wanted me to visit." She tapped a square into the wall, then stepped through.

Kody went next, then Bubba and Xev. Nick followed and slammed against a solid surface.

Cursing, he rubbed his forehead that had hit the wall.

Before he could do anything else, an arm reached from the other side, and yanked him through it.

He gasped and prepared for war, until he saw it was Kody. "Nice prank, guys. My nose and head thank you."

"Sorry." Xenia bowed her head sheepishly. "It only stays open for a few seconds. My grandpa didn't want anything following me in."

"Close, were you?" Bubba asked.

"No. I stayed away to honor my father. Contrary to lies others tell, I didn't venture here. I knew better."

"How so?"

She smiled at Nick before she answered his question. "My parents were very lenient and wonderful. They denied me nothing. So when they told me not to come here, I knew they wouldn't do that unless they had very good reasons to keep me away."

Without another word, she led them toward the creepy building that had sharp spires towering toward the sky.

"You know, just once I'd like to see a happy Disney castle. Not something out of a nightmare."

"Disney has creepy castles, too," Kody reminded him.

"Fair point. But I'd like it to be Cinderella's castle. You know, something fun and happy with singing mice, and a mop that cleans toilets so I don't have to."

Xenia cocked her head. "You're the Malachai. When do you clean toilets?"

"Whenever my mom tells me to."

Bubba clapped him on the back. "Good man."

If only he felt like one. Sighing, Nick walked along the pathway that ran parallel to the castle. "Do your magic unlocking powers work on this?"

Before she could answer, a low growl sounded.

Nick froze. "Here, draggy draggy?"

"It's not the dragon."

His eyes widened. He lowered his tone to a whisper. "If it's not the dragon, what is it?"

Something hit Nick hard in the chest. It lifted him off his feet and slammed him ten yards away, flat on his back. Pain exploded through his entire body. He landed so hard that it knocked the air from his lungs and returned his form to human.

Unable to speak, he was too stunned to fight. All he could do was lie there as Bubba and Xev unsheathed their swords and made ready to battle.

Kody lifted her bow.

"Hold!" Xenia touched Kody's hand and lowered her aim.

Confused, Nick watched as Xenia crept toward the shadows.

"Hey there, little one." She reached her hand toward the hedges.

Nick had just pushed himself to his feet when she let out a scream and vanished. "What the..." He ran to where she'd been.

There was no trace of her or whatever had made that noise.

"Xenia!" Kody called.

No answer whatsoever.

Stunned, Nick looked at each of them in turn. "What just happened?"

"I think your draggy ate her."

He really didn't appreciate Xev's humor right then. No wonder everyone wanted to choke him when he was being facetious.

Nick pulled back the shrubs. "Anyone have a more productive idea?"

Kody took his hand and gently nudged him away from the bushes. "I wouldn't do that. We don't know if something grabbed her or if the shrub ate her."

She had a point.

Sliding away from the greenery, Nick ran his hand through his hair. "Shouldn't we try to find her?"

Kody opened her mouth to call out, then stopped herself. All that would do was alert the others where they were. "I don't know, Nick. On one hand, I say we search, but I doubt anything here would cause her harm."

"Something grabbed her," he reminded them.

Xev grimaced. "My Spidey Sense says that it was done to protect her from whatever is planning to attack us."

Nick groaned because he was probably right. "And my ulcer just had another baby. Thank you so much for that scary thought."

Bubba sucked his breath in sharply. "But he's probably right. My money says that she's back on her side, safely tucked into her own castle."

That actually made sense. Especially when he searched his inherited memories for a clue as to what had grabbed her, and nothing came to mind.

Nick scratched his chin as he examined the foliage around them. "For the record, I don't want to be sucked into a shrub."

Xev smirked. "Since Caleb isn't here, I feel compelled to provide one of his retorts. I didn't want to be sucked into another one of your misadventures in Hellscape, either."

"Ha ha." But Nick was leery of anything green. "Y'all really think she's back home?"

They nodded in unison.

Honestly, it made more sense than he wanted to admit. And at least she'd been here to get them inside. Maybe that was an automatic reaction to Grim finding her on his grounds.

She got caught, and the alarm system threw her back over the wall.

He'd go with that.

Nick looked around to get his bearings. "She said that Ash was in a garden around the back, right?"

Xev nodded.

Nick gestured at the path over his shoulder. "So, this way?"

"Unless they changed it, yes." But there was no missing the reluctance in Xev's eyes.

"When was the last time you were here?"

"I don't want to think about it, kid." Xev rolled his shoulders as if they burned.

That made Nick feel like a total jerk as he realized that the last time Xev had been here must have been when they ripped his wings from him.

Crap. The last thing he'd wanted was to make Xev relive that nightmare. In spite of their banter that sometimes held good-natured barbs, he loved his great-grandfather. They'd been through a lot together, and he knew that Xev would always be there for him.

Before he could stop himself, he hugged Xev. "They were the assholes. Not you. You didn't deserve what they did."

Xev gave him a hard squeeze. "You're all right for a nasty demon."

"Yeah, yeah. Remember that the next time you want to slap me." Stepping back, Nick headed down the path. Cautiously. The last thing he wanted was to run into the dragon.

Or another man-eating shrub.

And as he went, he whispered a quiet prayer that Xenia was all right.

He took deep breaths as he looked all around and waited for the next ambush. Gah, no wonder his mom complained about stress. It was exhausting. He much preferred being the thing everyone feared than being the one waiting for something terrifying to attack.

And on that note...

He returned to his Malachai body.

Kody slowed. "Something wrong?"

"Not yet. But I'm sure that'll change. I'd rather be prepared than caught off guard."

"I was just thinking that." Xev looked up at the walls. "Xenia told us that Grim knew we were here. Why hasn't he attacked?"

"Maybe he was the bush that grabbed her." But Nick knew better even as he said that. The shrubs were too subtle for Grim.

Nah, Old Man Grim would tangle them with the shrubs and then set fire to them. Rain down acid and brimstone.

Make their heads explode.

Yeah, that was more Grim's style. The bloodier the better. Make them sweat and enjoy watching them squirm. He was sick that way.

Nick glanced around. "Anyone else getting a bad

feeling in their stomach?"

"It's been more than ten minutes since your last meal, Nick. For you, it's probably hunger."

Bubba was right. He did have a hefty appetite.

Still...

Nick froze as they rounded the corner of the castle. "Huh. When they said statue in a garden, I envisioned a pretty little garden with a single statue of Ash looking like Walt Disney at Disney World. No one said it was a statue maze. How are we going to pick Ash out of *this*?"

They all drew up short beside him as he stared at what had to be a hundred statues or more.

"Wow," Xev breathed. "I haven't seen anything like this since Apollymi went wild on the Atlantean gods."

"Hey, now! That's my family you're talking about."

Xev cut a sideways stare at Kody. "I made no comment about your relatives, only that Apollymi went to town on them."

It was true. After the Greek god Apollo murdered Ash when Ash was in his human body, Apollymi had been freed from her prison. To say she became unhinged over the death of her son would be tantamount to calling Fuji an anthill. She'd cut a swath of slaughter through her pantheon and over the Earth to the point that Artemis had been forced to bring Ash back to life in order to return Apollymi to her prison.

No one wanted to relive that horror.

Except whoever had created this lovely monument.

Dang.

"Is this a family thing?" Nick asked Kody. "Do I have to worry about you getting angry at me one day, and going Medusa?"

"Not really. My grandfather pulls body parts off his family members and mutilates them. Sometimes for no reason whatsoever. God of Chaos. Gotta love him."

Nick winced at the reminder that Set was Kody's grandfather. And that he was renowned for his brutality. "Awesome. I just got another ulcer. It's now making nice with the one I got a few minutes ago."

Xev clapped him on the back. "Ah now, Nick. Why are you fretting? Your family's known to pull the wings off those who anger them. I'd pit Apollymi and Jaden up against Set any day."

Nick wanted to whimper.

Until he thought of something. "Wait... I would be related to Xenia, right?"

"Yeah. Cousins. Why?"

He smiled at Xev. "Then I should have the same ability to get into the castle?"

"Maybe."

Nick tsked at him. "Maybe's just a baby you rock until it's a yes."

Xev rolled his eyes. "Why do you want to go into the castle?"

"Hey, people pay lots of money to tour castles... and haunted houses. This is both. I like twofers."

Kody's jaw dropped. "Are you serious?"

"Nah. I was just curious." Nick headed for the statues.

Man, it was rough to look at them. Too many of them held expressions of terror or horror permanently etched into the stone. He couldn't imagine going about his business and then having some narcissistic jerkweed turn him into this.

He looked over to Kody. "What do you think they did to get turned to stone?"

"Probably nothing. Wrong place. Wrong time."

That wasn't comforting, given that they were currently trespassing.

Wrong place. Wrong time.

Nick swallowed hard, not wanting to think about that. So, he quickly changed the subject. "How are we going to find Ash among all these?"

"We split off and search."

Made sense. "I'll start here."

They had just stepped away from Nick when he heard a sudden hiss from behind.

"What are you doing in my garden?"

8

Nick froze, along with the others. At first, he didn't see anything.

Then a tiny...

No, it wasn't a dragonfly. Though that was what it first appeared. Only slightly bigger, it was an actual dragon flying. Surely this wasn't the fierce Were-Hunter dragon Xenia had told them about.

Was it?

Laughing, he wanted to reach out and pet the adorable creature that couldn't be any larger than his fist. "Hey, little guy. What are you—"

It blasted a ring of fire between them. A large one that was more akin to a flamethrower.

Okay, that was a different story.

Nick held his hand up and deflected the flames. "Whoa! Little fly, what are you doing?"

It fluttered in front of Nick's face. "Defending my charges. What are you doing here, Malachai?"

Nick considered lying to the dragon. But that wasn't his nature. Besides, with his luck, it'd know he was lying, grow bigger than a house, and eat him alive.

"We're looking for a friend."

The dragon floated to the ground and transformed into a teenaged girl with lavender eyes and bright red hair. There was something about her that reminded him of an impish elf. And this was definitely not what Nick was expecting.

"Who's your friend you seek?" she asked.

Kody frowned at her. "Don't you want to know our names?"

She shook her head. "If someone asks who was here, I'd rather be able to say I have no clue and mean it honestly."

That made sense.

Nick took a breath and answered her question. "We're here for Acheron Parthenopaeus."

She choked on a laugh. Until she realized Nick wasn't joking. "You're serious?"

"Absolutely. I need him."

"You don't need anyone. You're the Malachai."

Nick's blood ran cold at the sound of a voice that was all too familiar. In fact, it haunted his nightmares.

Grim.

His heart hammering, he turned around to face his old mentor... and flunky.

"Grim... It's been a minute."

Standing in full armor, Grim had his hair slicked back on his head. He'd grown a thick beard that made him look like an evil villain.

Nick tsked at him. "Way to stay true to the stereotype, *Jafar*. I liked it better when you looked like one of my teachers."

"And I liked it better when you were dead. Guess we can't have everything we want, eh?"

Guess not. Nick pulled out his Malachai sword and extended it. "How are we going to play this?" He figured Grim would charge forward to fight.

He didn't.

Instead, Grim slowly closed the distance between them and draped his arm around Nick's shoulders. "I feel like we got off to a bad start."

Every fiber of his being went on high alert. Grim was up to something. He knew it. He was *never* this nice.

"What?" Nick was incredulous.

Grim patted him on the back. "I know. I know. We've had our issues in the past. You disrespected me. I promised to kill you... but I think we should put that pettiness behind us."

Nick was aghast at his words. Pettiness? Seriously? The dude had promised to slaughter all of them and had tried his best to do it. "Did you accidentally inhale some fumes, old man? Fry your brain cells? Get hit on the head one time too many? What's going on here?"

Grim held his hands up. "Lots of things have changed since you died." He glanced around their group. "I don't even want to know how you and Nyria are back... or Xev. I won't even question it. I'm too grateful."

"Grateful?" Nick asked incredulously. How could Grim be grateful for the return of his enemies?

Whacking Nick on the back, he actually laughed. "Absolutely. Grateful to the gods that I have another chance to..." His voice trailed off for no particular reason. Almost as if he thought he was talking to himself, and then remembered that Nick and the others were there.

Clearing his throat, he stepped back. "Anyway, I am not happy with current management. I've realized that I might have made a mistake with my earlier allegiance, and as such... You wouldn't happen to be interested in renewing our old relationship, would you?"

Oh yeah... what?!

Was he hallucinating? Could those words have really just come out of Grim's mouth?

Nick was so baffled and confused that he didn't even know where to begin. "I thought you said I didn't need anyone."

"I was doing that for dramatic effect. Worked, didn't it?" He grinned at Nick. "And I hope you don't mind my removing Xenia from this. She can be a little... annoying at times. And the last thing I want is for her to interject her stupidity on what I think will be an incredible partnership."

He's nuts. Not that Nick didn't know that from all their earlier encounters, but still...

He held his hand up to Grim. "Can you give us a minute? I need to confer with my group."

"Sure." Grim moved closer to the statues. "Take your time. But remember, I'm on your side." He clicked his tongue and pointed his finger at Nick.

Uh-huh. Sure.

His mind boggled, Nick pulled his friends in the opposite direction. "Okay, guys. WTF! Anyone have any idea what to think about this?"

Kody shook her head. "Don't trust him. He's a liar and a beast who serves no one but himself."

Xev agreed. "I'm with Kody. Given everything we've gone through with him... We should stake him to the wall and leave him for dead. Whatever we do, we cannot trust him. He's evil to his core."

That was an odd thought coming from someone who'd once switched sides.

"Bubba?"

"I don't know. On the one hand, I lean toward Xev and Kody. However, people can change. It's possible he's seen the error of his ways. If he's really wanting to work with us, he could provide valuable intel."

True. Grim knew everything about Laguerre and Cyprian. She was his wife and they had been battle partners for hundreds of thousands of years.

But again, they had been partners and allies for hundreds of thousands of years. Together, they had devastated entire kingdoms and come close to ruling their world. They'd had children together.

Why would Grim want to join Nick and his crew, given all that?

Nick turned back toward Grim. "What exactly has happened to make you a turncoat?"

"Cyprian," he hissed that name like a curse. "He turned on us, and I want to see that little weasel burn."

That was something Nick understood, and it made more sense. Grim was all about revenge. It was the air the ancient god breathed.

Kody sucked her breath in through her teeth. "Nick, don't do it. We can never trust him."

He grinned. "I don't trust him, Kode. I do trust his selfish greed. He wants what we want. To take Cyprian down. My enemy's enemy is my friend."

"Or your end," she said firmly. "Remember the scorpion and the frog. Grim's nature is to sting."

"I know. You know. Bubba knows and Xev knows. As long as we watch him..."

Frustrated, she placed his hand over her eyes. "Damn you and your stubbornness, you Cajun toad. Fine, you've made up your mind. But when this ends badly, remember that I was against it."

"Duly noted." Nick moved to stand in front of Grim. "You want us to trust you? Free Acheron."

Grim paused as if he were debating with himself. Finally, he nodded and snapped his fingers.

Lightning came out of nowhere and splintered a statue in the garden.

Nick's heart pounded at the sound and explosion. "What did you do?"

"What you asked."

"I asked for Acheron back. Not for you to..." Nick's voice trailed off as he saw movement behind Grim.

His breath caught as the Atlantean god stumbled out of the debris. Almost seven feet tall, with jet-black hair that held a red stripe, there was no missing Acheron and those red flame biker boots and long black leather coat.

"Uncle Uh-Oh!" Kody ran to him.

Coughing and wheezing, Ash smiled as he saw her. "Neramou! What are you doing here?"

"We came to free you."

"We?"

She motioned to their group.

Acheron gaped as he saw them watching him. "Nick?"

Nick stepped forward hesitantly. "Yeah. You okay, big guy?"

"A little rattled. Excessively confused." Ash wiped the dust off his face. "Someone catch me up?"

Nick didn't know where to start. Thankfully, Xev didn't have that problem as he began filling in all that had happened over the last few years.

Ash took it all in stride until Xev got to the part about Grim. For some reason, that struck a nerve.

His swirling silver eyes turned red. "You're wanting to join us? After what you did? Are you kidding me?"

Grim stepped back. "I may have made some mistakes."

"May?" Ash growled.

"Okay, I made some mistakes. But together, we can fix it."

Acheron let out an evil laugh. "This isn't a tire that blew on the interstate. You've been making mistakes for centuries. *Grave* mistakes."

Grim paled even more. "I know. I know. But if you think about it, I'm just doing what I'm supposed to be doing. I served Adarian for centuries."

Nick scoffed at that. "You betrayed my father."

"I betray everyone." The nonchalance in his tone was appalling. He really didn't care.

Kody gestured at Grim. "Which is why I vote we not have him in our club."

Ash shook his head. "My enemy's enemy—"

"Exactly what I said!" Nick jumped in, cutting him off.

Acheron ignored him. "My gut says to slaughter you where you stand, Grim. My head wants to give you a chance. But if you betray us..."

"I'm dead." Again with the nonchalance.

Ash nodded. "And remember, I have the powers to do it. Immortality or not."

True. Acheron was a god-killer. He was one of the few beings who could kill a god without disrupting the universe. Kody's father was another one.

Which reminded Nick of what they needed to do next. "Styxx wouldn't happen to be here, too, would he?"

Grim shook his head. "Cyprian spread your group

out. Last thing he wanted was for all of you to join forces again. So he decided no one-stop shopping."

That made Nick's heart flutter. Was Grim saying what he hoped he was saying? "We can defeat him?"

"Together, yes. You almost defeated him anyway. Had he not killed Nyria in the fight, you would have kicked his ass into oblivion."

Nick actually sat down on the ground with that declaration. All this time, he'd assumed they were outnumbered and outmatched.

But they'd almost won...

"You okay, kid?"

He nodded at Bubba's question. "We can win."

"*You* can win," Grim repeated.

Those words echoed in Nick's mind as a thousand different emotions went through him simultaneously. For the first time in a long time, they had hope.

Then again, he almost hated that they had hope. It was a treacherous beast that kept people going, even when it was useless.

Of all the four-letter words in the world, he hated hope most of all. It was the meanest and cruelest.

Yet there it was, urging him to pick up the gauntlet and finish this fight. He had no choice.

I make my destiny.

And he was at a crossroads where there was no way

back. Everything had pushed him here. Stand and fight, or go home and lick his wounds.

He met Grim's gaze. "Is there any scenario, in any multiverse, where I save my mom?"

"You know the answer."

Sadly, he did. If string theory was correct, and given his own experience with venturing into a different dimension, his life had played out in every single scenario.

And in at least one of them, Cherise Gautier would be alive and happy. Why couldn't this be *that* outcome?

You have to try.

Aside from death and taxes, the only other guarantee in life was that if you didn't try, you'd never succeed. *You miss one hundred percent of the shots you don't take...*

Wayne Gretzky was right.

He heard someone tsking him. The moment she spoke, he knew that sing-songy cadence and weird words. "Now, now, Akri-Nick, don't be so sad and pouty-faced. Why you want to look like one of them mopey people who walk around all dour and weepy. Smile! You gots Akri-Kody. Akri. Akri-Bubba and Akri-Xev. All we needs is Akri-Caleb and we gots an army to eat all them nasty gods that make you sad. Even the heifer goddess!"

Nick gasped at the sound of a voice he'd never

thought to hear again. "Simi!" He shot to his feet to see the demon who had the same hair color as Ash. Only Simi's was pulled into two long pigtails.

Like Acheron, she held a set of fangs as well as wings she kept hidden. Right now, she looked a little older than she'd been twelve hundred years ago when they'd hung out. But she was still as beautiful as ever, with her sing-songy voice and unique views on the world.

"I have missed you so much!" He sprang to his feet to hug her. "How are you here?"

Ash pointed to his shoulder. "I didn't want to risk her fighting. She was a tattoo on my chest when I was frozen."

Yawning, Simi stretched. "And the Simi be so tired." Then her gaze went to Grim. With a feral hiss, she started for him.

Grim cringed and threw up a shield. "I'm on your side!"

Simi didn't care as she slammed against the invisible wall surrounding him. "Lemme in! The Simi is going to eat your head and liver, and she's not even going to use barbecue sauce!"

Ash pulled her back. "It's okay, Sim."

"Not okay! He kilt the Simi's boo. My children. I want him, Akri! Gimme his organs!"

Grim dared to meet her tear-filled gaze. "I'm sorry, Simi."

"Not as sorry as you'll be when the Simi gets her fangs on you!"

Acheron turned her to face him. "Breathe, Simkey. Breathe."

"No! I—" She broke off into tears.

Ash held her against his chest as he rubbed her back. "I know. I know. I feel the same hatred for him that you do."

"Then why's he not dead?"

"Because you need me," Grim said. "I'm the only one here who knows how Cyprian did what he did. Who knows where all the bodies are buried."

Nick hated to give him credit for anything, but Grim was right. They needed him.

"Fine," Ash growled. "Get me to Styxx, and if I can release him, we'll let you join our merry band."

"Deal."

One moment they were outside the castle, with the eerie statues, the next they were in what appeared to be a dungeon.

Nick shot into his Malachai form, then used his powers to grab Grim by the throat and pin him against the nearest wall. "What is this?"

If he'd betrayed them, Grim was dead. Splintered. So

dead, not even Artemis could bring him back.

Grim choked and held his hands up. "It's where Styxx is. Please... let me go. I'm helping. I swear!"

Nick wasn't so sure.

Acheron put his hand on Nick's arm. "Give him a chance to speak."

A tic started in Nick's jaw. His instinct was to splatter Grim all over the wall. But that was the Malachai speaking. His human part wasn't quite so gory.

So, Nick lowered him to the ground. "Speak quickly. Your life depends on it."

Still wheezing, Grim pushed himself to his feet. He used his powers to light the torches around them, then smirked. "You'd think someone would put power in this place, wouldn't you? But no. Let's keep the medieval torture theme going."

Nick scowled at his segue as Grim headed to an arched doorway that was barred with a locked gate. "What is this place?"

"One of Noir's prisons. It's a labyrinth. Styxx is in the center of it. You get to him, he'll be free."

"What's the catch?"

"You have to get to him."

It seemed deceptively easy. Which meant it wouldn't be at all. "How do I reach him?"

"Only you can figure it out." Grim glanced around to the others. "And you have to go alone."

Xev sucked his breath in sharply. "Nick—"

Grim held his hands up to cut him off. "The rules aren't negotiable. There are some doors and some things that everyone has to face alone. This is one of them. If you try to take someone in there with you... None of you will return."

Awesome.

Kody shook her head. "Don't do it, Nick. I don't trust him."

"Neither do I, but what choice do we have?"

Bubba's gaze narrowed. "We gut him and go in."

Simi flashed her fangs. "I like Akri-Bubba's idea. The Simi votes for that!"

Really, so did he. If only life worked that way.

But as he said, what choice did they have? "I'll listen to Grim. If I fail, feed him to Simi."

Her smile widening, she dug a bottle of hot sauce out of her coffin purse. "The Simi isn't hoping something happens to Akri-Nick, but she is hungry. Just saying."

At least she was honest. There was something to be said for that.

With a heavy sigh, Nick headed for the gate.

"Nick?"

He paused to look at Kody. "Yeah?"

"Be careful. I love you."

"Love you, too. Y'all watch over each other and I'll go get your dad."

She pulled him into her arms and gave him the sweetest kiss he'd ever known.

Nick breathed her in, grateful that she was a vital part of his life. Honestly, he had no idea what he'd do without her. Stepping back, he kissed her brow, then pushed her gently toward Simi. "Guard my girl for me, Simi. Don't let anything happen to her."

"I won't."

With a reluctance that ran through him, he released Kody and then faced the others. "If y'all hear me scream like a victim in a horror movie, please come get me."

Xev laughed. "Absolutely."

Nick inclined his head to him, then took a deep breath for courage.

Step through it.

But it felt so ominous. Terrifying. He couldn't remember the last time he'd fought alone. With no one at his back.

Honestly, he didn't want to go solo. It just didn't feel right.

Grim had no expression on his face whatsoever.

Just go.

Easier said than done. Nick knew he had to do it. But that didn't make it any better or easier.

You can do it.

He actually knew he *could* do it. The problem was, he didn't *want* to do it.

Closing his eyes, he tapped his powers and used them to light up the dark chamber. Then he moved his hand and broke the lock. The doors creaked even more ominously as he swung them wide with his telekinesis. He half expected an Alice Cooper song to start playing.

Where were those soundtracks when you needed them?

Then again, he started hearing Bauhaus's "Stigmata Martyr" ringing in his head. All this place needed was a wicked strobe and it would be the perfect place for a rave.

"Undead. Undead. Undead..." He began singing "Bela Lugosi's Dead."

It really wasn't helping. He could feel his ulcer growing as he waited for something to jump-scare him.

"I swear if that haggard old man jumps in my face, I'm going to rip his head off."

Think happy thoughts...

That would be Kody in a bikini. But not even that was helping. "It's a small world after all..." Nope, that song absolutely didn't work. In fact, it was creepier than his Bauhaus play list.

So, he moved on to his mom's favorite song. "I think I love you."

Wait, ew! He'd never before considered how utterly horrific that Partridge Family song was until now. Yeah, it would be a perfect serial killer theme. He could just see someone kidnapping a victim while singing it to them.

"Is there anything I can think of that's not creepy right now?"

"What are you afraid of?"

Nick froze at the sound of that unfamiliar voice. "Who are you?"

"Who are you?"

Truthfully, a scaredy-cat Malachai who wanted to run back the way he'd come. But he wasn't about to admit that to anyone other than the irritating voice in his head. "No one."

"What does No One seek?"

Nick came to a small opening that had three different paths he could choose from.

"I want to get to the center of this maze."

"Then choose your path."

Great. Now he was channeling Lady and the Tiger.

Pick the wrong path and he was sure there was something waiting there to eat him.

"Want to give me a hand choosing it?" he asked the unfamiliar voice.

"When all things are open for you, you have to select the one that seems best. No one can help you make that choice. It's one you have to pick, alone."

But he'd have to live with the consequences. That was terrifying. "I'd rather you pick so that I'll have someone to blame when it all goes wrong."

The disembodied voice tsked at him. "We are all responsible for the paths we choose. No matter what others say, or suggestions they give, only you pick the path. Only you bear the consequences."

"Not true. Whatever I decide will impact all the others in my life." Especially if he died. "The consequences will hit them just as hard. If not harder."

"You're right. So which one will you pick?"

He'd rather not pick at all. But that wasn't an option.

Closing his eyes, he tried to sift through his inherited memories. Had any of his predecessors ever been here?

Sadly, he couldn't find a single memory regarding any of this.

All he had to go on were his instincts.

You can do this. Do what Ash would do. Think it through.

Right and left looked good. His instinct was to go right.

Don't. Think about what you know of the gods.

Moderation. Never lean to the extreme. That was the one lesson that permeated so many stories. It was the thing Kyrian and Ash harped on.

In all things, moderation.

That meant the middle path. Always. He headed for it.

"Are you sure?" the unknown, unseen voice asked.

He was beginning to hate that voice. "Pretty sure."

"What if you're wrong?"

"I'll be screwed, won't I?"

"In ways you can't imagine."

Sighing, Nick shook his head. "You should work as a guidance counselor at my school. Pretty sure he gave me the same advice about picking a college and career. Abandon hope all ye who enter here."

And now he was hesitating.

Then he remembered what his mom and Kyrian always told him. *The worst mistakes I've made in my life were those I made out of fear. Never let fear control your actions. It's a horrible master.*

Granted, that was a paraphrase, as they each had

their own take on it. But that was the root of what they'd told him repeatedly.

Those who let fear rule them have fear for a master.

That wasn't him. It was the middle. He knew it.

Nick made up his mind and headed down that path, expecting the worst.

Nothing happened.

Good? Maybe? He wasn't sure.

But nothing had grabbed him yet, and the voice seemed to have faded. That alone made him feel better.

The path turned sharply right, then left and left again. He felt as if he were being turned in every direction. The lack of sound was really beginning to grate on his nerves.

"Where'd you go irritating voice that for once isn't in my head?"

No answer.

"Figures. Guess you had to go take a leak." Which got him to thinking... where would he go if he had to go?

"Yeah, I'm not liking this at the moment. Is there really no porta-potty? Outhouse. Something?"

Again, no response.

How aggravating and rude.

Trying not to think about it, Nick moved forward. At least nothing was attacking him. But maybe that was a bad thing. If the path was the right one, wouldn't flying monkeys or something equally as scary be trying to stop him?

Seemed reasonable, given his history.

Suddenly, the floor dropped out from under him.

"I knew it!" Nick used his wings to stay in place. He floated over a nasty pit of spikes and venomous snakes.

Had he not been in his Malachai form, that would have hurt.

No, that would have killed.

The only time he wanted to be a Nick-ka-bob was for Kody. She could stake him out any way she wanted, and he'd oblige her. But he refused to be demon kibble.

Flying away from the hole, he continued on his way.

Something came out of the darkness, headed for him.

"No, you don't!" Nick blasted it with his powers.

Then he used a fireball to light the way. He was a Malachai, after all. And he was making peace with that part of himself.

What choice did he have? He couldn't get rid of it. He'd seen that life, and it hadn't really been all that.

Being the Malachai did come with some perks... when people, demons and such weren't trying to kill, imprison, or control him.

But those days were over.

If you can't love yourself, who can?

Yeah, his mom was chock-full of great advice.

"I was listening, Mom." All those times she'd thought he wasn't, that he was ignoring her or rolling his eyes, he'd heard, and it'd stuck.

Are you really ready to embrace me?

That voice sounded so much like his father that it startled him. But he knew it was him and not Adarian. Wow.

Do I really sound that much like my dad?

Terrifying thought, given that he'd spent his whole life trying to be true to himself. Trying to be the complete and utter opposite of his father.

Maybe genes had more influence than he'd thought.

Nick came to another room. This one had five pathways to pick from.

Five. Six counting the one he was hovering in.

"Okay... give me a sign."

Nothing.

Ugh! Which way should he go now?

Trust your gut.

He wrinkled his nose at the Malachai voice in his head. *Trust his gut...*

Yeah, that was easier said than done. But to be honest, his gut was usually right. It was only when he second-guessed himself that he got into trouble. How many times had he done that and then berated himself for changing his mind?

The gut had a brain.

Trust the gut.

"Okay. But if you're wrong and I get in over my head, I will be pissed."

Nick opened his eyes and looked at the five different paths. His gut said to take the second one from the end on his left. He headed for it. "You better be right, gut."

His stomach clenched as he started down the path, waiting for something to jump out and attack him.

As he flew, he ran into something sticky, like a spider web. "Yuck!" Nick pulled at it, trying to get it off his face and bare arms. It was so gross!

Then he froze. What kind of spider would live in this place?

Uh, that thought sent shivers down his spine. He remembered Ash telling him stories about the Greek goddess who was half spider.

Actually, he didn't remember it. *I should have paid more attention.*

Why didn't I pay more attention?

"Um, Spider Goddess? If this is you and you can hear me, I'm a good Malachai. I don't smush your kin. I take them outside when I find them and set them free. We good?"

Nothing answered.

Maybe it was a regular spider. This wasn't Australia. Maybe things here were normal size.

"Why are you here?"

Nick flinched at the disembodied female voice. "Well, according to everyone who knows me, I'm here to strain their patience and irritate them."

"Is that supposed to be funny?"

"Only if you laugh."

The woman wasn't laughing.

Nick cleared his throat. "What about you? You just like to hang out in dark places?"

"I like to destroy invaders."

"I'll let you know if I see one." Nick hit something soft.

Oh crap! He held up his fireball, then wished he hadn't.

Yeah, this was the spider thing Kyrian had talked about. She had a wide black ball for her body and a little head with a million eyes on it.

And fangs. There were giant, icky fangs.

"Couldn't get an appointment with your hairdresser?"

The giant arachnid backed up. "Pardon?"

"Another awful joke, sorry." Nick let out a sigh. "Look, this is going to go one of two ways. I kill you or you kill me. How about we call a truce, and both go home happy?"

"Can't do that."

"Why?"

"My job is to make sure no one passes."

Nick flapped his wings. "My job is to kill and maim everything that crosses my path. You really want to do this?"

"You're the Malachai?"

"So they tell me."

The spider continued to eye him. Well, sort of. Some of the eyes were looking at him and some around him. It was really disconcerting. "I have a conundrum."

"Can I help with that?" Nick asked.

"Since you were the one who placed me here, maybe. I should eat you for that alone."

"Well, how about this? I set you free. Go build your web in a tree... or the throne room. Gross out the current occupants. How's that sound?"

She crept toward him. "You will let me go?"

"As long as you don't kill me, yes."

She came even closer.

Nick steeled himself in case it was a trap. "You thinking about it?"

"Is this a trick?"

"No. Are you tricking me?"

More of her eyes looked at him. "No. But how can I trust you? You've tricked me before."

"Lady Spider, I don't know you and we've never met. I swear. I wasn't the Malachai who did this to you. As I said, I don't pick on spider people. I respect y'all too much. Go Gwen Stacy!"

"Who?"

Nick grinned. "It's a comic book thing."

She cocked her head. "You are a very strange Malachai."

"So they tell me."

"I should attack you on principle. But you promise I can leave?"

"Sure. If you can find a door."

She bowed before him. "Thank you."

"My pleasure... What's your name?"

"Arachne."

"Arachne." The name Kyrian had given him. Made sense. "Nice meeting you. Sorry about your being here. Hope you find a warm orchard to spin in."

She inclined her head to him, then moved to leave.

"Hey, Arachne, before you go, can I ask you something?"

"Sure."

"I'm looking for a statue I was told had been put here. Have you seen it?"

"No. There's no statue in the labyrinth."

Nick gaped. If Grim had lied... "There has to be."

"There's not. I've been all the way through the labyrinth. No statues exist."

So help me, Grim. I'm going to gut you. Fury blinded him. Grim must have sent him on a suicide quest, knowing Arachne wanted to gut him. "How can I tell Kody that Styxx isn't here?"

The spider backed up. "Prince Styxx?"

"Yeah. He's the statue I'm looking for."

"But he's not a statue."

Nick blinked as shock ran through him. "Then what is he?"

"Perhaps I should show you."

9

Nick wasn't sure what he was expecting, but it definitely wasn't the pissed-off warrior chained to a wall.

Fury bled from every molecule of Styxx's body. He glared at him with an uncomprehending stare.

"What's wrong with him?"

"It's a spell."

Of course, it was. Nick let out a tired sigh. "Any idea how to break it?"

"No. You're the one who did it."

Which meant it was done by Cyprian. Apparently, Arachne couldn't tell the difference between them. And since he had the inherited memories of his Malachai ancestors, the only ones he lacked were Cyprian's.

That actually explained so much.

Like father, like son.

Gah, it'd be so helpful if the others were here. They, especially Acheron, might have a clue as to how to help Styxx.

"Styxx? Do you know me?"

He didn't speak. Rather, he lunged at Nick with a sword.

Nick jumped back and let out another exasperated sigh. How could he cure someone of a spell he hadn't created and one he had no idea about?

I hate you, Cyprian.

"What are you doing here?"

Nick gasped as he heard that familiar voice of his future son.

Like Beetlejuice, he must have said his name one time too many. Because here he was.

Full Malachai and ready to confront him.

Nick bowed up and glared at his hated offspring. "I've come to free Styxx."

"Can't have you doing that." Cyprian extended his sword.

One that was identical to Nick's.

How could that be?

"You have my sword?"

Cyprian smiled, exposing his fangs. "Took it off your rotting corpse after I gutted you."

Of course, he did.

But that reminded Nick of something. He wasn't growing weak in his son's presence. Weird. In the past, Cyprian had weakened his powers, and obviously, he'd weakened him when they'd fought and Cyprian had defeated him.

But now...

Bupkis. He was as strong as ever. It must be because in his timeline, Cyprian wasn't born or maybe because Cyprian had killed him.

Either way, the kid had no effect on his powers.

And that made him cocky. Nick motioned with one hand. "C'mon, punk. Let's dance."

Arachne pulled back.

Cyprian advanced on him with a vengeance. Nick parried his thrust and drove him back. "How did you beat me?"

"Because you're weak! Pathetic!"

Nick would give him that. He wasn't what he'd hoped to be. Still...

"I'm not the one hiding behind my mother's apron. Can't you do anything for yourself?"

That set fire to Cyprian, who began raining furious blows on Nick. He swung the sword, then blasted him.

Nick absorbed the blast. He let the pain feed his strength. Along with the unfettered anger. Now he understood his father. There was nothing like inhaling that sweet fury. It surged his powers so much that it made him dizzy.

It was heady and intoxicating.

Nick smiled at his son. "Blast me again."

That caught Cyprian off guard. "Pardon?"

"Hit me again. I dare you."

Cyprian pulled back. "What's wrong with you?"

"Nothing. I'm the Malachai."

A thousand emotions went over Cyprian's face in a matter of seconds. But the one he settled on was fear. That, too, increased Nick's powers.

"I killed you!"

"No. My fear did that. You struck while my back was turned." And after Cyprian had mortally wounded Kody. His attention had been on her and not his enemy.

This time, it was totally different.

"Now, you have what you've always craved. Your father's full attention. Enjoy it… son."

Cyprian cried out in rage before he attacked again.

Nick tsked at him. "That all you got?"

"Don't patronize me!"

"I'm your dad. Isn't that what I'm supposed to do? As my Aunt Mennie used to say, *If I'm not doing you wrong, then I'm not doing you right. I'm making you interesting.*

Because without me, you're just another snot-nose brat no one wants around."

"How dare you!"

"What? Speak the truth? Are you too sensitive to hear it?" Nick was fully channeling his own father now. And what scared him most was that he enjoyed the meanness. It tasted sweet on his tongue. "C'mon, show me how worthless you actually are."

Cyprian renewed the assault, but this time, Nick felt the boy's energy dipping.

He moved in for the kill.

Cyprian gasped as Nick's sword plunged through him. Gaping, he staggered back. "You can't kill me!"

"Apparently, I can. I did, if you remember."

Cyprian shook his head. "I will take everything you have. You're not going to survive me. I killed you once, and I will kill you again!"

Nick lunged forward, intending to end it.

Cyprian vanished.

Cursing, Nick growled in frustration. What kind of sick game was this?

But with no idea how to finish it, he turned back to Styxx, who was growling like a mad dog.

"Arachne?"

She didn't answer, and he didn't blame her for leaving. This had nothing to do with her.

Fine. It was his mess. He'd have to clean it up.

If only he knew where to start.

Other than getting a pissed-off demigod out of a labyrinth where he could come across more monsters, get lost, or get killed by his future father-in-law.

"My life really sucks." And the saddest part— he didn't see it getting any better.

10

By the time Nick found his way out with a snarling, rabid Styxx who'd fought him every step of the way, no one was in the garden.

"What the hell, people?" Where had they gone?

"Malachai?"

He stopped as he heard the little dragon's voice. "Hey. Where's everybody?"

Her eyes turned sad. "The evil Malachai came and took them."

Nick's heart stopped. "Wait? What?"

She nodded. "We were waiting for you to return when he came out, screaming. Before anyone knew what he intended, he took them."

"Took them where?"

She shrugged.

Nick cursed himself for the stupidity. Grim must have betrayed them, after all. "I can't believe I let Grim dupe us!"

"He didn't betray you."

Nick was incredulous. "What?"

"He tried to fight the others and was wounded."

That stunned him to his core. Grim had stuck to his word. Wow. The world must be ending for real.

Growling, Styxx lunged at him.

Nick stepped aside. "Can you please stop doing that? I'm your friend."

Then again, Styxx lunging at him with a sword reminded him of how Styxx had behaved when he'd found out Nick and his daughter were dating.

Why did he remember that?

It was hard to forget a giant man trying to strangle the life out of you.

SIGHING, Nick looked at the dragon. "I forgot your name. Sorry."

"You didn't ask my name. It's Alura."

"Sorry, Alura. I should have asked. Do you know any way to snap Styxx out of this spell?"

She moved over toward Styxx and whispered something into his ear.

Nothing happened, but at least Styxx wasn't trying to kill him.

"What did you do?"

"Something my mother taught me."

"Which is?"

Before she could answer, Styxx groaned and rubbed his head as if he were waking up with a migraine.

Alura smiled. "It's a special enchantment that can break most spells."

"Most?"

"There are some so powerful they can't be broken by anyone other than the caster or by killing the caster."

That was good to know.

Styxx looked at him with a fierce grimace. "Ambrose? What did they do to you? You look like you ought to be in diapers."

Nick laughed. "I'm not Ambrose yet. I'm Nick from high school."

Styxx ignored that as he looked around. "Where's Nyria?"

Nick glanced to Alura before he answered. "She's been taken."

Fury creased his brow as he curled his lips. "By whom? Where?"

"We don't know. But we'll find her." Nick wished he felt as confident as he sounded.

"The who part," Alura said, "was Cyprian. I've no idea where they might be."

"But you can find out," Styxx said to Nick.

Nick arched a brow at that. "What?"

"Reach out to Nyria like you used to. She'll respond."

It took Nick a second to realize that Styxx was talking about his future self. "I've never reached out to her like that."

Styxx opened his mouth, then closed it as a terrifying shoebill flew down and landed between them.

Nick grimaced at what had to be the ugliest bird he'd ever seen in his life. No wonder they called it the death pelican. Honestly, pelicans should be offended.

Craning its neck, it stared at Nick. "Malachai, I have your loved ones, and I look forward to killing them again." The bird began to scream. Only it wasn't the bird's voice.

It was Kody's.

His heart pounding, Nick glared at the bird that was obviously Cyprian's messenger. "Stop it!"

"If you want me to stop torturing them, renounce your powers to me."

Was Cyprian insane?

He started to argue that he couldn't do that. Then he remembered when his father died.

Adarian had passed his powers to Nick so that he could save his mom after his father died.

That meant that he *could* hand over his powers.

However, there was one problem. He didn't know how. That memory hadn't been passed over to him. Nor did it make sense given that Cyprian would have taken those powers at Nick's death.

Right?

Yeah, right. Cyprian already had his powers. Why ask for them again?

Well, if you're that stupid, far be it from me to educate you. Rather he'd play the game and see if he could win.

"You have to let my family go first."

Kody's scream echoed louder.

Nick's heart skipped a beat as he decided that he didn't want to play this game with someone who was obviously insane. "Stop! Don't hurt her. Tell me where to meet you."

"Come inside."

Said the spider to the fly... Nick had always hated that tale. Now, he hated it even more as it echoed in his head.

The hideous bird flew off.

He glanced at Styxx. "You think Cyprian knows you're cured?"

"I don't know. Want me to pretend I'm still enchanted?"

"Can you?"

Styxx returned to being obnoxious and going for Nick's throat.

Then he stopped and returned to normal. "Pretending I want to kill you is easy. You dated my daughter."

"I married your daughter."

"Not helping me not want to rip out your throat."

Nick took a step away from him. Given that Styxx was a legendary commander who had basically defeated Atlantis by the time he was Nick's age... he deserved respect. "Did I ever tell you what a great father-in-law you are?"

"Only when you wanted something."

Nick picked up the chain that was still holding Styxx. "Here, puppy, puppy. Let's go save Nyria."

"I'll help." Alura turned back into a dragon, then made herself so small that she was able to fit on Styxx's red cloak as a brooch.

Wow. She looked so much like metal that Nick had to reach out and touch her.

"You're tickling me."

He jumped away from her. "That's amazing."

"No. Amazing is when I'm too big to fit in the castle."

Yeah, okay. A massive dragon could come in handy.

Still not sure they should be doing this, Nick led Styxx inside.

He paused to take in the aura of Nouveau Evil that permeated the dark decor. The walls and ceilings were lit by the entrails of luminescent demons. Even better? The walls were decorated with the bones of those who'd pissed off Noir and Azura.

No wonder his father had escaped and vowed to never return here.

Styxx jerked hard at the chain.

"Hey!" Nick warned. "I might need that arm later. Try not to break it."

Styxx responded with a fierce growl that sounded authentic.

In fact, it was so real that Nick wondered if he needed to leave him chained someplace.

"Are you pretending still?" Nick whispered.

Of course, I am. Styxx sent the thought into his head.

Thank, God!

But dang. The man could be a little gentler.

"Hello?" Nick called. "Where's the great evil I'm here to quash?"

Lights flashed before Nick was jerked through a wall, into Noir's old throne room.

His father's memories tore through his mind. He saw Adarian being dragged in here and chained to his master's throne. Worse, he felt his father's surge of hatred and pain.

Yet it was his own outrage that rose to push the other emotions aside.

Cyprian sat on Noir's throne, glaring at him. "How nice of you to bring me another playmate. I'd forgotten how much I loved hearing the twins scream."

Nick snorted at that. "Knowing Ash and Styxx, I doubt there's anything you could ever do to make them flinch, never mind scream."

Both of them had survived hell in their lives. Pain was second nature to both.

And still Cyprian snarled at him. "You know you can't win. I've already killed you."

Nick glanced to the blood where he'd wounded Cyprian. "And I killed and wounded you. Guess that makes us even."

"You cheated!"

"So did you."

Cyprian came off the throne, shooting god-bolts at him. Nick let go of Styxx to protect him and moved away so that Styxx wouldn't be collateral damage.

"You can't win."

Nick shook his head as he returned fireballs. "You keep saying that, and yet, somehow, here I am."

Roaring, Cyprian ran at him.

Nick used his powers to shove him into a wall. "Where are my friends and family?"

"Kill me and they all die."

That took the fight out of Nick. He refused to go up against Cyprian if it meant harm to them.

Cyprian moved to the side of the throne, where a red cloth was pooled on the floor.

A bad feeling went through Nick.

One that was confirmed when Cyprian used his powers to yank the cloth back.

Kaziel lay there, covered in blood.

Tears filled Nick's eyes as he felt himself go weak. Unable to handle it, he sank to his knees. He wanted to scream out, but no sound would leave his lips.

How could Kaziel be dead?

How!

Even Styxx went still.

No. No. No!

Cyprian blasted him. "How many of them do I have to kill? Give me your powers or I'll kill them all."

Kody's scream rang out.

"She's the next one I'll take."

Nick felt his Malachai powers surge. "You are such a brat."

"Am not!"

Well, that proved that.

Fury flowed through Nick, making him stronger. And that made him want to taste the blood of his son. To feast on Cyprian's entrails.

Like a Malachai would.

"You want my powers? Come get them."

Greedier than any creature should be, Cyprian flew at him.

Over and over, Nick saw the chaos and blood this beast had sown. The chaos and blood he intended to sow in the future.

"You can't fight me and win," Cyprian snarled.

Maybe. Maybe not.

That wasn't the point.

Survival was.

Nick held his arm out to Cyprian. Electricity crackled around his red and black skin. "You want my powers?"

Cyprian all but salivated as he took Nick's arm.

And Nick unleashed his full fury against him.

The force was so great, it threw Cyprian against the farthest wall. "You think you know pain? Son, you've no idea. Physical pain is nothing. Anyone can survive that. It's mental anguish that is the most brutal and destructive." Nick stalked toward his son. "You know *nothing* of that pain. Nothing. Because the only way to feel it is to care about something more than yourself."

Whimpering, Cyprian tried to crawl away, but Nick wouldn't let him.

"It was that soul-deep anguish over her daughter that caused Laguerre to curse us for eternity. But you..." Nick picked him up and slung him with his powers to the ceiling, then down to the floor. "You will never know the power I wield."

And for the first time, Nick understood Adarian. Why he'd been so strong at the end.

Love.

Nothing was more painful than to have it ripped from you, especially when it was taken by a monster.

"Where is my family!" Nick roared. "Tell me or I'll tear you limb from limb."

Something hit Nick like a bolt of lightning.

Hissing, he turned to see Laguerre behind him. "I am the Ambrose Malachai!"

"And I'm the daughter of Noir." She blasted him again.

Nick staggered back as more pain ripped through his body. "You can't stop me from fulfilling the curse you placed on us."

Tears actually welled in her eyes. "Son kills the father."

"Or the father kills the son."

She shook her head. "Not today."

Nick shot a blast at her, but she dodged it and ran to Cyprian.

Just as he sent another blast toward them, she vanished, taking Cyprian with her.

Aghast, Nick tried to track her through the aether

. But she left no trace whatsoever.

"Are you kidding me?" He wanted to taste their blood. To feel Laguerre's heart in his fist.

Until he saw Kaziel's body. That zapped all his fury from him.

His heart broken, he staggered toward the wolf, then sank down on his knees. Tears welled in his eyes as he remembered all the times Kaziel had saved his life.

And this was how he'd repaid him. Death. Nick sniffed as his tears began.

He felt someone behind him. Assuming it was Styxx, he didn't bother looking. He was too consumed by grief.

"Let me." It sounded like Styxx until he saw out of the corner of his eye that somehow it was Ash.

Stunned, Nick sat back and looked around at his family. They were all there.

Kody moved to lean against him and gift him with a tight hug.

"How are you here?"

Grim sighed. "I was able to bring them back once Laguerre left. She doesn't know I've defected... yet."

Nick looked to Vawn and Aeron. "I'm so sorry about Kaziel."

Ash scoffed. "No need to be sorry." He stood up at the same time Kaziel did.

The wolf shook his white fur, then yawned widely as if he'd been asleep.

Nick laughed as he remembered that Artemis took her powers to restore life from Acheron. As the final fate, Acheron had the ability to flip death off. "I thought you didn't believe in interfering with fate."

Those swirling silver eyes were piercing. "I'm the final fate. Screw those bitches. We're playing by new rules now." His gaze went to Kody. "And they've pissed me off."

Styxx nodded. "We need to reassemble our army. Most of all, we need to find our families." His gaze turned dark. "I have to find Bethany."

Ash nodded in agreement. "And Tory, and our children."

"Exactly." Styxx offered his hand to Nick to help him to his feet, then he glared at Grim. "Where has Laguerre gone?"

"I don't know. Probably to Noir and Azura. It's where she'd feel safest."

Nick sighed wearily. "So, we lost."

"No," Vawn said firmly while stroking Kaziel's fur.

"We've sabotaged Cyprian. He knows he didn't win. We're still alive and he wasn't able to siphon any of your powers."

Kody nodded. "We know where we screwed up in the past."

"And we won't make those mistakes again," Acheron said.

"No," Nick agreed. "We'll find all new ones to make."

Caleb held his hand out to Nick. "One for all?"

Xev shook his head. "No. Us for the world."

Nick placed his hand on theirs. "Never give up. Never surrender. Tomorrow, we fight again."

Armageddon was coming, and they were going to stop it.

EPILOGUE

Cyprian growled as he found himself back inside his mother's hovel. Okay, it wasn't really a hovel, but it was nowhere near as vast as Noir's castle.

"Why did you do that, Mother? I was winning!"

She gaped at him. "You were about to die."

"Impossible!"

She backhanded him so hard, he felt several of his teeth loosen. "Don't be stupid. Ambrose is fully capable of destroying you."

Cyprian wanted to argue, but deep inside, he knew she was right. "Then what do we do?"

She smiled coldly. "Our enemy's enemy."

He scowled. "How do you mean?"

"We are going to ally with those who hate Ambrose as much as we do. Trust me... Ambrose won't win. We defeated him once, we'll do it again. Only this time, we will destroy them all. One by one. Until they're all dead. Including Apollymi."

DARK-HUNTER®

Retribution

The Guardian

The Dark-Hunter Companion

Time Untime

Styxx

Dark Bites

Son of No One

Dragonbane

Dragonmark

Dragonsworn

Stygian

Deadmen Walking

Death Doesn't Bargain

At Death's Door

Born of Night

Born of Fire

Born of Ice

Fire & Ice

Born of Shadows

Born of Silence

Cloak & Silence

Born of Fury

Born of Defiance

Born of Betrayal

Born of Legend

Born of Vengeance

Born of Blood

Born of Trouble

Born of Darkness

Lords of Avalon

(written as Kinley MacGregor)

Sword of Darkness

Knight of Darkness

ABOUT THE AUTHOR

Defying all odds is what #1 New York Times and international bestselling author Sherrilyn Kenyon does best. Rising from extreme poverty as a child that culminated in being a homeless mother with an infant, she has become one of the most popular and influential authors in the world (in both adult and young adult fiction), with dedicated legions of fans known as Paladins–thousands of whom proudly sport tattoos from her numerous genre-defying series.

Since her first book debuted in 1993 while she was still in college, she has placed more than 80 novels on the New York Times list in all formats and genres, including manga and graphic novels, and has more than 70 million books in print worldwide. Her current series include: Dark-Hunters®, Chronicles of Nick®, Deadman's Cross™, Black Hat Society™, Nevermore™, Silent Swans™, Lords of Avalon® and, The League®.

Over the years, her Lords of Avalon® novels have been adapted by Marvel, and her Dark-Hunters® and Chronicles of Nick® are New York Times bestselling manga and comics and are #1 bestselling adult coloring books.

Join her and her Paladins online at QueenofAll-Shadows.com and www.facebook.com/mysherrilyn.

www.ingramcontent.com/pod-product-compliance
Lightning Source LLC
Chambersburg PA
CBHW020126120726
47903CB00007B/2129